EVERYTHING
IS AWFUL
AND YOU'RE
A TERRIBLE
PERSON

EVERYTHING IS AWFUL AND YOU'RE A TERRIBLE PERSON

DANIEL
ZOMPARELLI

ARSENAL PULP PRESS
VANCOUVER

ARSENAL PULP PRESS
Suite 202 – 211 East Georgia St.
Vancouver, BC V6A 1Z6
Canada
arsenalpulp.com

The publisher gratefully acknowledges the support of the Canada Council for the Arts and the British Columbia Arts Council for its publishing program, and the Government of Canada (through the Canada Book Fund) and the Government of British Columbia (through the Book Publishing Tax Credit Program) for its publishing activities.

This is a work of fiction. Any resemblance of characters to persons either living or deceased is purely coincidental.

"Ghosts Can Be Boyfriends Too" was first published in *Joyland Magazine*, February 2, 2016.
"His Birthday Is Not March 7th" was longlisted for the CBC Short Story Prize, 2016. "Slips" was shortlisted for the Cosmonauts Flash Fiction Contest, 2015.

Cover and text design by Oliver McPartlin
Edited by Susan Safyan

Printed and bound in Canada

Library and Archives Canada Cataloguing in Publication:
Zomparelli, Daniel, 1985-, author
    Everything is awful and you're a terrible person / Daniel Zomparelli.

Short stories.
Issued in print and electronic formats.
ISBN 978-1-55152-675-1 (softcover).--ISBN 978-1-55152-676-8 (HTML)

    I. Title.

PS8649.O66E94 2017   C813'.6   C2017-900896-X
                                             C2017-900897-8

CONTENTS

dad told me you were back at work, and i angrily went to find you. i was furious that you had left us alone for three years. when i got to your desk, everything was empty. i went back home and searched for a necklace you always wore and texted my ex, asking him to please take care of me, as i wasn't holding up so well. he told me to stop. i fell apart, and all i had left of you was your necklace.

GHOSTS CAN BE BOYFRIENDS TOO

I woke up, the feeling of empty weighing to one side of the bed. I heard Derek again in the other room, talking to himself.

"Remember that time we went camping and everyone caught us doing it in the forest?" Derek laughed.

The silence answered him.

"*Derek, you're sleep talking again!*" I screamed from the bed.

He went silent, came into the room, apologized, and went back to bed. This was the fifth night in a row. We had just moved in together, so I wasn't sure if this was normal or not.

In the morning, I asked him if he needed to go to a sleep therapist, but he declined. We spent the morning reorganizing the kitchen. He took breaks to call his mother and to reassure her that Jesus was not coming to take us away for our sins.

"No, Mom, we were not in church this week," Derek replied. "Mom, I'm not going to church, just get over it." He hung up the phone.

Derek had previously organized the kitchen, but he placed things in weird spots. Everything was alphabetized. Cereal went next to the Coca Cola, flour went next to the forks, soap was next to the sugar.

"Derek, you can't keep the poisonous stuff next to the sugar."

"Sugar is poison."

I nodded in agreement. I went back to reorganizing and started to move the pill bottles into one spot. Derek tried to argue with me, but I didn't think it was smart to have random pill bottles everywhere. Some of the pill bottles were unlabelled; I asked him to label them so that we didn't mix them up. He refused, so I labelled them with the names of the things they sat between, like "bran / breads," "mint tea / napkins," "Pringles / protein powder," etc.

When we finished, we ate leftover pizza and watched a show on TV about a chef who was going restaurant to restaurant explaining to the owners why they should just shut down unless they let him help them. One restaurant was pirate-themed, and the servers dressed in costume. The chef turned it into a bar and grill called "Corporate Bar and Grill." The owners cried tears of joy as more and more customers poured in, until there were too many of them and they overwhelmed the restaurant. Money was falling out of the restaurant's till, and the servers' tips were falling out of their pants. I woke up with Derek asleep on my lap. I shook him awake, and we crawled into our bed.

In the middle of the night, I heard him talking again about how I had moved everything in the kitchen.

"Derek, you're talking in your sleep again," I groaned.

Derek turned to me and stood up immediately. He had a disgruntled look on his face.

The night rolled around me, never letting me sleep. Derek continued to talk in the other room.

"I can't say that *Showgirls* is the best movie, but of course it has its high points."

There was a silence.

"No, Nomi Malone is not supposed to represent socialism, that doesn't make any sense. I guess she could possibly represent poverty and the difficulty of being a woman."

There was a silence.

"Sure, if you like having sex like a blow-up mattress being rapidly deflated."

Another silence.

"Are you ever going to forgive me for that? You left. I mean, you were dead. What was I supposed to do?"

I walked into the room. Derek looked at me as if I was interrupting. He got up, walked to the bed without saying anything, and promptly fell asleep.

In the morning, we continued to organize the living room. I put out all of my comics and figurines, and Derek followed behind me and put them in boxes.

"I don't want your figurines out. They look ridiculous."

"This isn't just your home." I grabbed my figurines out of the box.

"Fine. But you can only put out three. I don't want people to think I'm dating a child." Derek could tell I was upset, so he came and rubbed my back, kissed my forehead, and whispered, "a very handsome and funny and smart child."

We finished by noon, and there was only one box left, labeled "Jared." I went to open it, but Derek grabbed my arm.

"No, that one is going to my mom's place. We don't need to open it."

"Who's Jared?"

"Just an ex-boyfriend."

"Can I at least see what's inside?"

"No. Just leave it."

That night we went out for the first time in weeks. We started at the nautical-themed pub across from our apartment. I ordered a grog, which was a margarita and beer served in a sand bucket. Derek ordered a water. The server said we looked familiar and gave us a free basket of onion rings they called "float tubes."

We moved on to the club down the street, and I drank beer until Derek came back from the bathroom and said he wanted to go to the bar down the street. At the last bar of the night, Derek came back from the bathroom, dancing goofily, and I started to laugh uncontrollably. He continued to dance toward me, so I stopped him. "Derek, since when do you dance this much?"

He didn't respond and kept dancing. I tried to get his attention, but his eyes searched the room. I told him we should head home, and he nodded in agreement. As we walked home, Derek kept stopping to shake his butt at me. I remembered how light he was, like he couldn't touch the ground. I wanted to hold his hand so that I could anchor him to the ground. I felt so heavy, but sometimes he lifted me off the earth when we were together.

He slept through the night, or at least I was so drunk that if he woke up, I didn't notice.

I made us coffees and brought one to him in bed. Derek had post-drug sadness in his eyes.

"You were really high last night." I put the sugar next to his coffee.

"I know, it was lots of fun."

"It just felt weird. You didn't look like yourself at the end of the night." He rolled away from me and ignored his coffee.

When he finally woke up, I could hear him talking to himself. It escalated into shouting when I heard a door slam. Derek ran out of the bedroom crying. He grabbed his coat and didn't return until the evening.

When he finally got home, he started to pace back and forth in front of me.

"Okay. So, I know you're going to think I'm crazy, and this always happens, but I need to tell you something, okay? And you have to promise you won't think I'm crazy, because everyone always says that I'm crazy and leaves, and I just can't deal with that right now, okay?"

I assured him that I wouldn't call him crazy and would be fine with whatever he had to tell me.

"So, you know that boyfriend I had a long time ago that died?"

I nodded and put my hand on his knee.

"Well, he's haunting this house. But, like, not haunting."

I continued to nod.

"See!? You already think I'm crazy! Look at you."

"I was just nodding." I pulled him into a hug and comforted him. We sat and talked for several hours while he recounted everything from Jared's death to the first time he saw him as a ghost. Now, Derek told me, Jared comes back every year around this time to ask Derek to get back together.

"I can't do it. I can't date a ghost. But I still love him so much."

I gently patted his back. "I'm right here."

"Sorry," he mumbled into his hands.

"What if we just focused on me and you. This other guy, this, uh, ghost, he'll just have to deal with it. Okay?"

Derek nodded and rolled his body into my lap.

///

I woke up and noticed Derek's spot was empty. I could hear mumbling coming from the other room. I grabbed my glasses and shuffled into the living room.

"Derek, come back to bed."

"I can't. We need to talk."

"Is everything okay?"

"No. Well, yes. But also, no. Yes and no, if that makes any sense."

"No, it doesn't."

Derek began to sniffle, and his body started to shake, which meant he would begin crying if I didn't calm him down. I rushed to his side and rubbed his back until he stopped shaking.

"I—I need to leave you."

I stared blankly at him.

"I am leaving you for Jared."

I stared blankly.

"We've been seeing each other in secret." There was a pause. "It's ... I didn't expect this. Can you say something, please?"

I tried to calm down, but burst out, "Jared isn't real! If you want to leave me, just leave me. Don't fucking make shit up about ghosts."

"You promised you wouldn't call me crazy!"

"I never said you were crazy. I'm sorry, I shouldn't have phrased it like that. I just don't want you to leave."

I calmed down and asked if Jared could come into the room and talk to the two of us like adults.

"He can't just float into the room like some sort of fairy. He's a ghost."

"I'm sorry, I don't know as much about ghosts as you do," I said, uncertain if I was being sincere or not.

The conversation went like this: Derek and Jared talked for a few hours as I watched. It was three in the morning when I suggested that we try a relationship that involved the three of us. Derek's eyes were glowing; he loved the idea. I told myself that it was only a ghost—not like we were getting into a three-way relationship with a poltergeist.

So Jared officially moved in. Derek opened up the box he'd been keeping hidden from me. It contained Jared's belongings: his toothbrush, his cardigan, a necklace, some old notes. We put his things out and even made room for him in the bed. We started to set a place for him for dinner, and like clockwork, when I'd leave the room to go to the bathroom, his meal would be eaten and Derek would be cleaning up after him.

I was hesitant at first, but dating a ghost had a lot of upsides. Jared would sneak off into other apartments and tell us exactly what the other neighbours were doing. Whenever either of us were upset with a co-worker, Jared would agree to haunt them for the evening.

One evening I came home with a Ouija board, excited about this gift for Derek, but it only made Jared angry. He said that it was insulting to ghosts and that I was probably "ghost-racist."

Jared and I never talked directly; Derek was always our translator, and I could usually tell where Jared was because Derek would lock eyes with him. The way he would intensely stare at one position in the room almost made it possible for me to see Jared—like a silver outline would form. Derek was more than happy to communicate between us. We only fought a handful of times when we accused each other of taking up more of Derek's time. It quickly escalated into a series of insult-throwing fits, in which I called him a "Casper-looking motherfucker," and he called me a "useless flesh bucket."

The first time we tried a threesome, it was awkward. Derek kept shifting me, saying that I was sitting on Jared. I felt a cold breeze against my skin where Jared and I pressed against each other. Sometimes I just sat back and watched as Derek wove his body with Jared's; I could almost see Jared's outline through Derek. Sometimes Derek would direct Jared and me; we were never very good at being together without Derek, but we both tried to make it work. Derek would yell, "You're not even trying—you're on opposite sides of the bed!" and, "You look ridiculous; you're just jerking off the air. Jared is over here."

One evening, the three of us went out to the nautical-themed bar. I'd already had too many grogs to go anywhere else, but Jared wanted to go somewhere new. Derek promised me we would go home soon. When we were walking, Derek sped up. I yelled at him to wait for me. When I caught up to him, I was walking too fast, so he yelled at me to wait for him. Then he rushed past me and turned left into a dark street. He didn't come home for another hour. He crawled into bed and mumbled an apology. Then Jared rolled in around five in the morning, and Derek apologized for him.

When I woke up, Derek was already bent over the counter taking a bump of coke.

"You're not supposed to be doing cocaine to wake you up in the morning," I said.

"Why not? It has the same chemical effects as caffeine." He stared at me with a look of complete confidence in what he was saying. "It's just the conservatism of society telling you that one drug is better than the other."

"I—uh, I never thought of it that way." I took a small line, and it quickly woke me up.

Soon we were going out every other night. The same routine repeated itself: As we were heading home, Derek would disappear into the dark. Later, he'd sneak into bed and apologize, followed some hours later by Jared, and Derek would apologize on Jared's behalf.

It was one month later when Jared's dinners stopped disappearing during my routine bathroom breaks. Derek looked at me, frowning.

"Jared isn't eating."

"Does he not like my cooking?"

"Maybe. He's been really mad at me lately."

We continued our routine, but the dinners continued to go uneaten. Derek would leave them out overnight. For a week, he left the dinner there to prove a point to Jared about how rude he was being. The food grew mold, while ants and fruit flies made the meal a home.

Later that week, I woke up in the middle of the night. The bed was empty. I could hear yelling in the living room.

"What did you expect?"

Silence.

"I can't!"

Silence.

"I know you can't just find a body, it's impossible. I'm trying to understand you, but you're asking too much from me."

Silence.

"Because I love him too much."

Silence.

"If I did that, how am I supposed to know where I would end up? Then I would lose you and him."

Silence.

"I just don't think I have it in me. I can't do it."

I sneaked back into bed; I'd been eavesdropping on a conversation that wasn't meant for me. When Derek came back to bed, I made extra room for Jared. Derek was weeping.

The next morning, I made the three of us breakfast. Derek split Jared's food between the two of us, then calmly stated, "He left us."

I looked up at my figurines. In the centre was Harley Quinn. I looked at her grin, the way she held herself. Poison Ivy stood next to her. I shouldn't have felt abandoned and rejected by a ghost, but it was just as painful as I remembered heartbreak to be.

That morning I went to the comic book shop. I picked up as many new comics as I could and even picked up several figurines. When I got home, I put them out. Three figurines didn't feel like enough. I always felt safe when I saw them, like they were protecting our home. They were heroes who would fight for justice even when justice wasn't on their side. I waited for Derek to argue with me about the figurines, but he didn't say anything. Every morning I would wake up and put out another figurine until the room was covered in tiny replicas of human beings in bright clothing wrapped tightly around their muscled bodies. Derek still refused to recognize their existence, like they were an audience of ghosts for our relationship.

A month later, Derek left me too. One evening he disappeared with just a bag of his clothes. He'd left behind Jared's belongings. Derek left without a note, and he never called me again, never tried to reach out to me. But I never tried to reach out to him. Something told me there would be no point.

A month after that, I found out from a friend of a friend that Derek was living in Toronto. He had found a new boyfriend within days of arriving and already moved in with him.

I wanted to tell him that the day after he left, Jared came back. I could tell because from then on, the leftovers from dinner would disappear in the night. I put out all of his things from his box, intermingled with my figurines. I think he liked this because after I did this, I found the Ouija board on the counter with the planchette pointing toward "hello."

Now we're trying to learn to speak to each other without Derek to translate the spaces in-between.

DATE: WHAT'S HIS FACE

Ryan arrived late at the coffee shop. He saw what's his face staring into an empty cup of coffee.

Ryan did his routine: he jumped into the seat across from the guy, pretended that he hated the place, and then dove into conversation. After a few moments, what's his face was trapped in the dialogue.

Every time Ryan made a joke, what's his face would fall into a fit of laughter, a high-pitched squeal. The laugh became nauseating to Ryan. It was as if it was coming from somewhere else, or as if it was a physical object on the table that was too repulsive to bear. Ryan looked down at the table, attempting to hide his disappointment.

They moved on from the coffee shop and slipped into a bar for a few drinks. What's his face slid his fingers up and down his chilled glass, removing the condensation. Their conversation floated around job titles, failed night clubs, failed past boyfriends, failed Grindr dates.

Ryan stared intently at what's his face, taking in every feature. His eyebrows were perfect. He could stand a nose job. Ryan noticed the breakouts in the corners of his forehead.

"You're kind of weird," Ryan smirked.

"Why?"

"I can just tell. There's something weird about you." Ryan, three beers in, began his ritual flirtation device of insulting his dates.

"You don't know me."

"Oh, I know you. I can tell."

What's his face became irritable. "Maybe I should go now."

"Why don't I walk you home."

What's his face looked up in confusion and agreed, not completely understanding why.

They arrived at what's his face's apartment lobby.

"What, do you live in a slum?" Ryan laughed.

What's his face scowled.

"Are you going to show me your place or what?"

What's his face let Ryan in.

THE GARDENS WERE HARDLY LUSH

Calvin H.

3/3/2016

[★]

Me and my boyfriend, now my ex-boyfriend, visited this so-called "hotel" this past weekend, and it was a disaster from the get-go. I'm not normally someone to write a bad review, but I have to say, this was the *worst* hotel I have ever been to.

Let's start with the service.

First, we were *barely* greeted when we walked in. I had to wave in someone's face even to get our bags carried to our room. My boyfriend was so embarrassed at the whole situation.

Next, we saw the room, and it was half the size the photos said it would be. We were pressed against each other the whole time, so naturally we were getting into a lot of fights. You can't just pack people into bunkers and not expect them to turn on each other. I complained right away, but no one cared that the room was basically a matchbox.

On the first night, we tried to go to sleep, but there was this couple next door having sex so loudly that it felt as though they were in our room. I could hear them screaming and moaning in pleasure. It was awful. We tried to complain about the sound, but no one answered my calls to the front desk.

I also noted that the gardens were described in the hotel write-up as "lush," and let me tell you, those gardens were hardly lush. I know a lush garden when I see one, and yours are *not* lush gardens.

On the second night, my then-boyfriend and I were fighting almost every thirty minutes. We decided that maybe we should go for the mid-day wine meet-and-greet in the lobby. What a mistake! We sat down, and immediately one of your staff poured us this disgusting, vile mouthwash. I immediately complained, and my boyfriend was very upset about the whole thing. He said he was so embarrassed, but I refused to let that piss poison touch my lips. I've heard of bad wine before, but come on, that was the "lush" gardens of wine.

Later that night, the loud sex was back. I mean, did they even take a break from their orgasms? I can't even imagine sex like that. It was like Moaning Myrtle had set up shop next door.

Finally, and this was the worst of it, the last night, when we ordered your "Romantic Evening For Two," everything fell apart. The masseuse showed up sixteen minutes late. She was unapologetic about her lateness, and my boyfriend was so upset at me. He tells me that I'm controlling. But who shows up late for a "Romantic Evening for Two"? Since when is being late "romantic"? So I was just sitting there, getting told that I was controlling when I couldn't even control a hotel to do its shitty job.

Then our champagne and chocolate showed up, but by then we were in a full-blown fight. How was champagne and chocolate going to fix this? You couldn't have brought the champagne on time? And the bellhop was just staring at us while we fought, waiting for a fucking tip. And then my boyfriend said that I was angry all the time. So I turned white with rage and threw the champagne across the room, because I resented that. I could barely afford this fucking bed and breakfast, as I was in-between jobs. I had used the last of my savings for this! Of course I was fucking angry. And I thought this was finally going to be the relationship that lasted.

So we got home and broke up, and I remembered those "lush" fucking gardens. How is anyone supposed to be in love in a hotel that was more like a torture game? I saw ALL of the *Saw* movies, and I'd much rather have cut off my arms than stay at your hotel. All I wanted was one weekend with my boyfriend, and it was completely ruined by you.

And maybe you should look up the definition of "lush" while you're at it.

DATE: CHILLANDLAIDBACKDUDE

What's up?

Not much, just got back from the gym. :p

What you up to tonight?

Just chillin'.

You live around here?

Yeah, downtown. It's pretty chill here.

:)

:p

;)

What you up to?

Nothing. Was thinking about going out. You have anymore pics?

Yeah, sure.
[12.jpg]

[lastnight.jpg]
You've got a lot of tattoos.

Yeah, it's all good.

[pic1.jpg]
[pic2.jpg]

[meandjonatpride.jpg]
[morningfun.jpg]
[bentover.jpg]
[nutbind.jpg]

*You have unread messages from a
user that you have blocked*

PROGRESS

I was putting paper tacks up in my cubicle and trying out different shapes. I was working on a pirate ship being sunk by a giant octopus. I ran out of blue tacks, so I turned to go to the storage room when I heard the beep of an email arriving in my inbox.

Co-worker 1 used to send me daily emails with sad faces; the number of sad faces equalled how many hours were left in the workday. In the last hour, he'd changed that to minutes, and then seconds when it was close to five p.m. We recently used the sad faces to mean the number of days left in my contract. Boss 2 had made it clear that my job was done when the contract was over. Boss 3 made it clear by posting my job position on the office website. Boss 4 never came to the office, so I didn't know how he felt about it.

blank@officetime.com: X grabbed my ass again. Not sure why no one is calling it sexual harassment.

>me@officetime.com: Did you report it?

>>blank@officetime.com: No ☹ I need this job for another few weeks and I don't want to stir anything up. Plus I heard someone reported him before, but no one cared. I guess it doesn't count if a guy is doing it to a guy.

>>>me@officetime.com: I'd tell him to go fuck himself next time.

>>>>blank@officetime.com: I did, he said only if I watched.

>>>>>me@officetime.com: lol, that's pretty funny.

>>>>>>blank@officetime.com: ☹ ☹ ☹ ☹ ☹ ☹ ☹ ☹ ☹ ☹ ☹ ☹

To fill in the time at work, I began to take photos of myself with different emotions to see what I looked like when I was sad, happy, surprised, etc. They all kind of looked the same. I began to organize them in folders labelled sad, happy, surprised, etc. I took the photos every day to see if they were different and put them in a hidden folder on my computer titled "Progress."

Co-worker 6 stood over my shoulder one day as I was taking a sad face photo. "Are you working?" She smiled.

"Yeah, just testing out the webcam for my computer. It was being weird."

"Well, I fixed the scanner, so you can finish whatever you were trying to do before."

I nodded. I'd been scanning portions of my arm and zooming in to see the hairs.

"Isn't it funny how we hire people with degrees, but then they end up doing work that anyone with a high school education can do?"

I nodded, then watched Co-worker 6 head into her office. She was the snack hoarder. Every day someone would bring in a snack for the whole office, usually doughnuts. Co-worker 6 would always grab a few doughnuts or whatever was the snack of the day, eat one, and hide two in her stash cabinet. She also had a keen sense of smugness that made me like her.

An email popped up that said someone had brought in salt-water taffy from their recent trip to Halifax. I slowly made my way to the office kitchen. When I arrived, Co-worker 2 was talking about being cyberbullied the week before. She'd been tweeting about the Beyoncé concert and some guy harassed her, saying Beyoncé wasn't even a real person.

"I used to cyber all the time," I said. "One time I cybered with a guy in an online *Family Feud* game."

"How does that even work?"

"The avatars were all seated on this couch, and one of them kind of looked like they were sitting on my lap, so I mentioned that and—"

"Please stop." Co-worker 2 sat back in her chair and sipped her coffee. I got up and went back to my desk. We had a report due on the new reporting system, so I still needed to fill in the empty paragraphs where I had written, "write something."

I would usually write something, then copy and paste that paragraph into each blank space of the report. I would reword each paragraph so it didn't look like I was repeating myself, but the idea always was the same. *The reporting process needs to be looked at more closely.*

I logged online to read the local news. There was another article on the local housing crisis. *Fuck.* My head began to pound. I found the author of the article's Twitter account and tweeted: *Moronic.* They blocked me within minutes. I could feel the sweat ring around my hairline. *Fuck.*

blank@officetime.com: ☹ ☹ ☹ ☹ ☹ ☹ ☹

Boss 2 looked up from her desk, her hands placed firmly in front of her like she was preparing to be mounted. "I'm sorry, but this report is completely nonsensical. It's like you wrote some random jargon and then filled in the blanks, last minute." I noticed that her breasts were being squeezed by her shirt. I stared blankly at Boss 2.

She wore very tight clothing, which was distracting for the three straight guys in the office. Meanwhile, the only thing I usually noticed was that she wore cheap underwear. (The labels were sometimes visible from her light-fabric skirts.)

"You're going to have to write this again."

I stared blankly at her.

"Listen, I know you're going through a lot of stress, so maybe I can just help you out with this."

I stared blankly.

"Why don't you send the file to me, and I'll fix it up for you."

I nodded. "That would help me out a lot." I strolled back to my desk. I sat down and gripped the arms of my chair. Rage crept up slower than usual. I closed my eyes. I thought about disappearing if I pressed hard enough in my chair.

blank@officetime.com: ☹ ☹ ☹

I had only a few days left to take more Post-it notes. I'd collected several boxes of them in my closet at home by that time, but I figured I would need them since I wasn't going to have a job soon and Post-it notes were expensive.

Co-worker 1 was reading through reddit pages and sending me his favourite inspirational quotes, the most recent being, "Feelings are a gateway to our hearts, which is a journey to love."

I logged in to Twitter, where someone was posting about more funding for the arts. I tweeted at them to get a job like the rest of us. The rage boiled in my stomach, I didn't know what it was, but I typed furiously until the person blocked me. Meanwhile the office was still buzzing from the latest firing of an employee. There had been three firings in one week. Apparently someone was stealing office supplies.

Co-worker 3 came up to my desk to ask about the theft. I steered him off-topic by asking about his latest vacation. He'd gone to Disneyland, where he spends one week every year. This year he took his girlfriend. He's thirty-six. This is his first girlfriend.

I nodded my head as he excitedly described seeing the Disney characters and going on each ride. A pang of jealousy rose in my stomach. I couldn't figure out what it was. It twitched my abs. I excused myself and went to the coffee shop for my second break of the day.

I turned on my phone and went online. *Fuck. Fuck. Fuck.* Logged in and began to slide down the updates. Every update felt like an attack. *Oh yeah, this is* exactly *what we should invest all our money in.* Rage covered my body; sweat covered my forehead. *She should have tried harder.* Blocked.

blank@officetime.com: ☹

I opened the email from Co-worker 1. It was just the image of an ocean wave and the quote: "Love is happiness. Full stop." *The ocean doesn't give a fuck about love*, I thought.

Boss 1 took me into her office and began her speech about what a great employee I had been and how sad it was to see me go. They had already planned my party, which involved a cake left over from the previous employee's farewell party. There had been so many in that month that one cake now had to last for four different parties.

The entire staff came together in the conference room. It was a ritual that the entire staff showed up. Mostly because the entire staff really wanted cake.

Co-worker 6 was standing near the cake, and Boss 1 was pretending to listen to her story. Boss 1 stopped once she saw me, ushered me to the front of the conference room, and asked me to say a few words.

"Uh, thank you for having me," I said. I took a bow.

The staff stared awkwardly at me, so I moved toward the table that had the sparkling apple juice. The office wasn't against real alcohol, but that was too expensive, so a few of us kept beer and wine in our desks. I pretended to pour myself a glass of sparkling juice and then walked back to my desk to pour in the wine.

The staff rarely went back to work after an office party, except for the bosses. They would pretend they were working by sitting on their desks and drinking sparkling juice, which they had replaced with bourbon after the party. I walked into Boss 2's office for our afternoon meeting about the new letterhead we needed. Several of the male workers were listening as she talked about her latest trip to the Okanagan. There was a weird twitch in my abs as she described the winery where she'd stayed.

Boss 2 asked the other workers to leave and closed the door. She looked at me with sad eyes.

"I'm sorry you're leaving."

I nodded in response. She did look genuinely sad. I coughed awkwardly and pulled out the letterhead options.

"No, no. I'm not making you worry about this. Someone else will order new letterhead. I just wanted to talk with you on your last day. Any plans after this?"

I didn't really know what to say. I hadn't actually thought of any plans except to take my unemployment insurance and stay away from work for several months.

"I think I might take some time to learn a sport or try knitting."

She laughed, which shook her breasts. I tried not to stare at them. She walked around her desk and picked up a gift bag. She placed it gently in front of me.

"Is this for me?"

"Of course! I had to get something for you on your last day."

I opened the bag and found a few packages of Post-it notes in neon colours, a batch of office pens with the corporate logo on them, and a small flask. I murmured a thank you, and she gave me a strong hug. My hands dangled at the sides of my body. She laughed and said I needed to work on my hugs. She made me try again, told me not to be afraid of squeezing too hard. "Everyone loves a good strong hug," she said.

We tried again, and I did my best to squeeze her body. I felt a cold sweat coat my forehead. She laughed and said that it was a good start.

We stared blankly at each other for a moment, and then she looked down at her feet. After a couple of minutes, I grew tired of the silence and went back to my desk. I opened a Word document. I copied and pasted the statement "I feel weird" over and over again until it filled 3,000 pages, then I clicked print.

I pulled the Post-it notes out of the gift bag. Without thinking I started to write "goodbye" on each one with a sad face, and I posted them on all of the office computer screens.

When I was putting the Post-it on Co-worker 1's screen, he stopped me and said he wanted to show me something. He walked me toward the bathroom. When we got inside, he pressed into me and awkwardly kissed my mouth. I kissed back and slammed him against the wall. He fumbled to get his hands down my pants. I pulled him into the bathroom stall, and he quickly dropped his pants. He said he had this planned for my last day. We locked the bathroom stall and made no attempts to stifle the noise. No one came into the bathroom, or at least we were so distracted, we never noticed.

When we walked out of the stall, we saw a felt pen on the ground. Someone had drawn a few happy faces on the door of the stall. It looked like a half-finished sketch with gaping spaces between the happy faces. I picked up the pen and drew sad faces in the empty spots.

When I finished, Co-worker 1 was still washing up in the bathroom. He turned to me and said, "You know no one likes you here, right?"

I nodded and looked in the mirror. I couldn't tell if I was smiling or frowning.

DATE: MUSCGUY

Ryan parked his car just a block away from the address given to him. He didn't want to let MuscGuy know what his car looked like.

He strolled up to the door and buzzed to let himself in. MuscGuy had a deep voice, or the call system deepened his voice, or he purposely lowered it when he answered. "'Sup?"

MuscGuy opened the door wearing faded denim jeans disintegrating at the edges, a hoodie, and an old undershirt. He looked like he'd just woken up after a long shift at a construction site, but he smelled like honey-melon body soap, and there wasn't a speck of dirt on his perfectly manicured hands.

Ryan was about to comment on his fruity scent, but MuscGuy stopped him with, "So I guess you just got here after work or something?"

"Sorry, what?"

"It's just you look like you didn't get time to shower."

"No, I had time to shower, I—"

"Oh, sorry, I guess that's just how your hair looks normally."

Ryan flattened out his hair and took off his jacket. They moved into MuscGuy's kitchen, which was several different tones of grey and beige. There were a couple of framed posters of Vancouver scenery in varied tones of greige.

"So what do you do?" MuscGuy hovered over Ryan and stood extremely close.

"I, uh, work as a server."

"Just a server? Sorry, that was rude. I mean, do you want to be just a server, or are you working on something better?"

"I don't know. I was thinking about going to school. You?"

"I have my masters in Urban Studies, and a masters in History."

Ryan felt a cold sweat break out over his entire head. "I'm actually going back to school soon."

"Oh, yeah, for what?"

"Biology or maybe Engineering," he lied. Ryan's fingers twisted into knots. MuscGuy noticed, so Ryan flicked them out. MuscGuy walked over to Ryan and began to unbuckle his belt. He kissed Ryan on the forehead, then gripped the back of his neck.

"Do you want this?"

Ryan nodded. MuscGuy lifted Ryan up and carried him to the bed. Ryan didn't realize how much smaller he was than MuscGuy. Ryan relaxed and let him take control. MuscGuy pumped lube from an economy-sized bottle. Ryan nervously chuckled as he put it to his lips to taste. He hated the way the lube had a sweet taste but knew not to say anything. MuscGuy had a strong grip; he held Ryan tightly in every position. Once he was inside Ryan, MuscGuy gripped his back and massaged his upper shoulders. Ryan closed his eyes and imagined someone else, and then someone else, and continued to shift to another person. His mind flipped to a new person each moment. He opened his eyes, and the image disappeared, floated up. MuscGuy whispered into his ear, "Do you want it rough?" Ryan nodded but whispered "slow." MuscGuy whispered even more quietly, "I will make you feel so safe" as he tightened his grip around Ryan's neck. It went on like this all night. At one a.m., MuscGuy rolled over to see the time.

"Shit, you better go," he said.

"Would it be okay if I stayed the night?" asked Ryan.

"That doesn't work for me. I have work early in the morning."

Ryan nodded and put his clothes on. MuscGuy walked him to the door. Once he was outside, Ryan texted him: "Thanks, let's do that again." A bubble popped up that showed MuscGuy was writing a text, then the bubble disappeared. The text never showed up.

Ryan sent three more texts the next day. MuscGuy responded once. "Listen, not looking for anything, but if you wanna play again let me know."

BLOCKED

I took a photo of myself with my wine in the airplane.

See ya later bitches. #vacation #gayboy #toronto #ineededthis

I sat against the window and hoped no one was going to join me. Just before take-off, an older woman sat down next to me, and I let out a sigh. She kept the light on throughout the entire flight as I tried to sleep. She offered me gum, but I ignored her.

When I arrived, I waited for a cab. I turned on my phone and scanned through the nearby profiles. Swiping left, swiping left, swiping left. Too young, block. Too old, block. No face, block. I went through each profile, reading the "about me" as quickly as possible. This guy was not interested in drama. This guy was not interested in foreplay. This guy was not interested in hookups. This guy was not interested in Asians, but he wanted to make it very clear that he was not a racist. This guy was only interested in masc men.

The cab driver looked through the rearview mirror, "You here for vacation or for work?"

"Both, I guess."

"You a writer?" He nodded toward the unbound scripts piled next to me.

"Yup."

The cab arrived at the house on Palmerston Boulevard.

"That's good. Reading is good. My wife is a writer, of poetry. Not here, but in India."

"Could I read some of her poetry somewhere?"

"Yes, but it is all in Punjabi."

He told me his wife's name. I pretended to type it into my phone. I paid the cab driver and walked down Church Street.

When the cab driver asked if I was a writer, I'd lied. It was just something I did. Whenever anyone asked me an outright question about myself, I would lie. If they asked me a leading question that I knew was false, I would say it was true. It was a gag I was trying out. I wanted to see how much I could get away with. I wouldn't have to worry about consistency either because it was Toronto, and I could easily be swallowed up by the size of the population. I looked around, found the closest Church Street sign, and took a photo of myself next to it.

Made it to Toronto. #funtimes

///

I took a photo of myself in my outfit using the hotel mirror.

Night out. #findmeahusband #gayboy #toronto

A few guys were at the bar looking toward me. I smiled. My server came up and placed a beer in front of me and let me know that it was coming from them. I lifted my glass to them and smiled. The three of them walked over and sat at the open seats around my table, and we were quickly engaged in a fast-paced conversation. They were from here, they said. I told them that I wasn't but was planning to move here and wanted to try it out. They were working in marketing for separate independent firms. I was in-between jobs but wanted to get into acting. My agent had just dropped me, but I lied and said I'd left her. They asked if they would know me from anything I'd been in. I said, "Just a few commercials ... and maybe some of my YouTube skits and videos."

"Wait, you're that guy who recorded his breakup and posted it online!"

"Yeah, that's me."

"Wasn't that kind of mean?"

"Whatever; people are broken up with all of the time." I was irritated.

"But your boyfriend, he was devastated, or at least that's what it looked like. I could never do something like that."

"But you watched the video, didn't you?"

"Yeah, so what?"

"Did you share it with anyone?"

"Yeah, I posted it on Facebook."

"Well, now who's mean?"

He smiled. I ordered another round, after which the rest of his friends left for another bar. After a few more drinks, he asked if he could take a selfie with me. He clicked a photo and began filtering it to post online.

"Can I tag you in this?"

"Of course."

We had one more drink before he leaned in to kiss me and ask me to come home with him.

While we walked to his apartment, I took a selfie with him. I was too drunk to properly take a photo; it was blurry and mostly just specks of light from the street.

He pulled me into a hug on his oversized bed. We had a long kiss, and I grabbed for my phone.

"What are you doing?"

"I wanted to take a photo."

"Of us kissing?"

"Yeah, it would be great for my Instagram account."

He turned me on my side and kissed my back. I felt the sweat of our bodies pool between us, and I remembered what it felt like to have this. The apocalypse was waiting for us outside, and we would hold on as long as possible.

"Do you want to stay the night?"

"Yes," I lied.

In the middle of the night, I slipped out of bed and grabbed my clothes. He called out for me and asked where I was going. I said, "the bathroom," and then sneaked out the back door.

I walked back to the club where the last few men were stumbling out. Cabs were lined up, waiting on the street.

When I was in the cab, I posted the selfie of us kissing.

Toronto Romance #love #lovewins

The cab driver spoke up:

You like going to these kind of bars?

Yup.

Me too, but I'm shy.

It's good to get out there.

Sometimes I will go to those bars too. And I will hug and kiss a man, but nothing more. They always want more. They always touch me more.

Do you sometimes want more?

Yes, but I'm afraid.

Why?

I don't want my heart broken. I'm scared. My friends tell me to follow my heart, but I follow my brain. What should I do?

I stopped talking and looked at my phone.

///

When I got into the gym bathroom, I took a photo of myself in front of the mirror with a hand towel covering my bum.

#legday

I checked the photo a few times before I made it to a small coffee shop. 3.2k likes. Not bad in just under half an hour. I ordered two croissants and grabbed a handful of napkins. The server brought them on a plate.

"No, sorry, can I get that to go?"

"No, you stay here, with me."

"I can't." My reply sounded more tired than flirty.

"No, with me. It's so cold outside."

He held down the plate with the croissants and stared at me like it was a duel. I imagined him as the candlestick character from *Beauty and the Beast*. I was the sexy duster that he wanted to woo. I stared back at him. I wanted those croissants, and I didn't want to stay.

"I need my croissants. I can't stay; I have a very important business meeting," I lied. He put the croissants in a bag, frowned, and asked if I would come back.

"Of course. I just moved in down the block, so you'll see me almost every day," I lied again.

I've always imagined that when you lie, you create another world where that lie exists. Each time I lie, there's a version of me who goes on to be or do that thing. One of me will go on to live here and go to this coffee shop every day. Maybe that version of me will fall in love with the coffee-shop owner. Settle down. Maybe help him open a second shop. Each lie breaks this world into small pieces, turning into a new story, breaking and turning into new stories until all you're left with is the small bits. Nothing you can hold on to.

///

The bartender, unprompted, placed a beer in front of me.

"This is for you, you don't have to have sex with me."

"Okay, but what if I did want to have sex with you?"

He responded with a confused look on his face.

"Is there, like, a sex amount of beers, or are you only offering non-sexual beers?"

He smiled.

I took a photo of myself with a cute, grumpy look on my face.

Bitches get free drinks. #fuckit

My phone rang. It was my old agent. She talked excitedly about taking me back on. I was hesitant, but she said she had a deal for me and to book a flight home. I yelled over at the bartender, "I'm not going to need this free beer—get me something better than that!"

///

You like going to these kind of bars?

No.

I do, but I'm shy.

Okay.

Sometimes I will go to those bars too. And I will hug and kiss a man, but nothing more. They always want more. They always touch me more.

Okay.

Aren't you afraid?

No.

I don't want my heart broken. I'm scared. My friends tell me to follow my heart, but I follow my brain.

I nodded.

So then what should I do?

I got out of the cab.

///

I was invited to a small Halloween house party through a friend of a friend. I wasn't really prepared for a costume so I threw on a plaid shirt and said I was a lumberjack. It was open bar, so I went pretty hard on the vodka. I kept eying the man dressed as Winnie the Pooh throughout the evening. He was mostly trying to avoid me, so I pushed a little more for his attention, and finally cornered Winnie the Pooh into a conversation:

"I run a small company," I lied.

"Really?" Winnie the Pooh asked. "What's the business?"

"I sell inflatables."

"Like sex toys?"

"No, don't be stupid. Like inflatable cars to car companies or like inflatable bananas to banana stands. I'm one of the largest sellers in the inflatables world around Canada, or the IW as we like to call it," I winked.

He faked a smile.

"You know, Winnie the Pooh never wears pants," I said.

"So?"

"Well, why don't we try that out in my hotel?" I leaned in to kiss him, but he remained unmoved. I began to stick my tongue into his mouth, but he wouldn't respond; I could feel his closed teeth with my tongue. He backed away.

"Maybe you should have dressed as Eeyore instead of Winnie the Pooh," I slurred as he ducked into the kitchen.

I took a blurry photo of Winnie the Pooh from afar.

Dick.

///

You like going to these kind of bars?

Yup. But it's never busy like this in Vancouver.

Me too, but I'm shy.

Me too.

Sometimes I will go to those bars too. And I will hug and kiss a man, but nothing more. They always want more. They always touch me more.

Do you sometimes want more?

Yes, but I'm afraid.

Why?

I don't want my heart broken. I'm scared. My friends tell me to follow my heart, but I follow my brain.

I always follow my brain, but that gets your heart broken too.

So then what should I do?

My real and honest advice?

I opened the door to leave.

Have your heart broken.

///

I swiped left, hit the block button, swiped left, hit the block button. One man messaged with the question, "Do you have a hotel? I can't host, but I think we could have a lot of fun together."

"Sure," I replied "come find me."

"Which hotel?"

"The Marriott, room 432," I lied. A few minutes later, I blocked him. I imagined him going to the hotel and finding the parallel version of me, waiting for him in a robe. Letting him stay the night.

///

I sat at the bar. When I looked up, I saw a handsome man staring at me. I asked the bartender to send him another round of whatever he was drinking. The bartender dropped off his drink. The guy asked who bought it and the bartender pointed at me. I raised my glass high.

"Really?" the guy yelled.

"Yes," I hollered back.

The guy grabbed his drank and sat down next to me.

"You must not remember who I am."

"Oh, have we already chatted online?"

"No. You forced yourself on me two nights ago. I was dressed as Winnie the Pooh."

I paused and sipped my beer. "That's not how I remember it."

"Okay. Well. Either way, thanks for the drink." He got up and walked away.

"Wait! I'm sorry. Please, just sit down for a drink."

He looked back at me with a defeated look, which I knew meant he would come back for the drink. He sipped from his beer and walked back to the seat next to me.

"Fine. I'm going to sit and finish this drink with you, but could you at least be real with me."

"I'm always real."

He laughed. "Oh yeah, like that inflatable company bullshit you gave me? I know you. You're that guy with like a million Instagram followers, and you broke up with your boyfriend via YouTube."

"I was just joking around about the inflatable company. Listen, I've had a lot of problems in my life, so maybe I joke around to make up for it or something."

"Oh yeah?"

"Yes, like, I have a really troubled past."

He laughed. "I don't think you know what a troubled past is."

"I've had a very hard life, nothing you would understand."

"You don't know me, and it sounds like you don't know what a hard life is, and from what I've gathered from the very short time I've talked to you, I think I can guess that you're a privileged fucking white boy who was handed everything he wanted in his life."

"Well, you don't know me at all, so you're fucking wrong."

"Okay, then you clearly have enough time to Instagram every waking moment."

"That doesn't mean anything, and that's bullshit to say."

"You know what? Fine. I can't hate on that. But how about breaking up with your boyfriend online?"

"You don't even know if that was real or not."

"Either fucking way, that's cold. Why would you even want to pretend like that was okay?"

"I think people put too much weight into that. So what? Everything online is fake anyway."

"Some people use social media to find community and to find a voice, to amplify people who are oppressed, so they are heard. You can't just act like the internet is some toilet for you to piss in."

"I don't owe anyone anything, and I think it was smart to see something real online."

"So it was real."

"Yeah, so what?"

"So that's fucking terrible! You broke someone's heart just for the fucking likes!"

"YouTube is my career, okay? I needed to do that. It's not like every job is always so straight forward."

"But you could have some integrity or maybe some fucking talent. That's why you posted your fucking breakup online, because you're so desperate to be someone without doing any of the work. By stepping on someone's heart. Being a little prick won't bring you any happiness." He slammed the beer and walked away.

I gave him the finger until he was out of sight. I looked at my middle finger in the air; it looked much smaller than I assumed it was.

I took a photo of myself with my middle finger.

Fuck it. #gayboy #instagay #life #love #haters #toronto #fuckit

I hailed a cab, jumped in, and slammed the door.

"You like going to these kind of bars?"

Ryan sat on the park bench three feet from the beach concession stand. He was a few minutes early, but he was making sure he would be able to enjoy the sunset on the Seawall.

_____ was running late. The sun balanced just above the ocean. He apologized for being so late. The sun dipped into the ocean.

He wasn't going to come. Ryan held his phone in his pocket. Anticipated the phone's vibration.

I LOVE PIE

"Ruin a sunset."—Dina Del Bucchia

It's sunset. I dig my feet into the sand, sip cold wine. Not great wine, but good wine. We share some hummus and bread. Not good hummus and bread; actually, terrible hummus and bread. I look up to see his smiling face.

"This is perfect," Darryl says.

I shake my head in a way that says yes and no at the same time.

It's this sunset.

He rolls to his side and asks for a sunset kiss. I agree. I've been kind of waiting for this kiss for a while. As his lips press against mine, I notice his tongue pushing quickly through, and then I feel his tongue searching my mouth. Intensely engaging my mouth, almost cleaning my teeth.

"Perfect," he whispers.

I nod.

He takes a giant bite out of some bread and hummus and rolls back into a sigh of delight, "Oh, yum!" He smiles at me. "This is so good. I can't believe how good this is. Do you love it?"

I nod in a way that says yes and no at the same time.

He takes out his phone to take a photo of the sunset. I take my phone out too. He snaps a shot of the sunset, and I snap a shot of him taking a photo of the sunset.

"We should go back to my place," he whispers.

We get back to his place, and everything is clean. The bathroom is spotless, the kitchen is bare, and all the furniture has perfect clean lines. Clean, knee-cutting, shin-breaking lines.

I push him quickly to the bed.

He crawls up my body, smiling, kissing me from toe to face. When he reaches midway, he looks up and says, "oh, yum."

I think about hummus and bread. I think about my genitals being replaced by hummus and bread. Like I could lie down at any Mediterranean restaurant and customers would say, "What a great appetizer for the whole family, and it's vegan friendly!" I keep myself quiet. Push the thought out of my head. He backs away from a kiss and sighs. "What are you thinking about?"

I smile and say, "You."

He puts his head onto my chest and quickly falls asleep. I take out my phone and look up the etymology of the word "yum." *"Yum" is just a word; it's like any other word. Merriam-Webster agrees that "yum" is a word. In fact, "yum-yum" is also correct word usage.*

We wake up the next day, the Saturday of Pride weekend. He's in the kitchen singing, I'm in the bed and can smell coffee.

"I put some coffee out for you, I know you like coffee."

"That's really nice of you," I say.

"What do you want to do today?"

"Well, it's Pride weekend, so I was planning on hiding in a straight bar all weekend."

"And miss Pride?" He looks at me as if I am joking.

"Of course. I always skip Pride. It's an awful corporate shill masquerading as a festival of equality."

"But what about the good it does?"

"Yeah, I'm sure it does a lot of good. A bunch of suburbanites looking at us like we're in a fucking zoo. Or all the hard-bodied men in speedos wearing glitter and logos."

"I don't know, that sounds a bit judgmental."

I feel a sting in my gut and go quiet. "Fine. I'll go with you."

The Pride parade comes and goes like a series of commercials fuelled by beer. We slip through beer gardens that turn morning into night and end up at a rooftop Pride party, drinking in the rest of the evening. Darryl is hopping from group to group, engaging everyone in conversation.

I can see him talking to my ex and my other most-recent ex. He's deeply invested in the conversation. Ryan comes up behind me.

"Are all your exes finally starting a support group?"

"Fuck off."

"Calm down, queen, it was just a joke."

A girl stumbles up to me. She looks as if she is having a panic attack.

"Are you okay?"

"No, I don't feel okay."

I grab her and pull her into a hug. She calms down.

"You're high, right?"

"Yes."

I rub her back until she calms down, tell her she is just feeling weird because of the drugs, and it will all melt away.

I leave her for a moment to refill my beer. My ex pours me a beer. I smile; he looks apologetic.

"I forgive you," I say.

"What?" He doesn't hear me—or believe me, I can't tell which.

"Nothing," I mumble.

*

"This movie is really interesting," Darryl says.

"What do you think is interesting about it?" I ask.

"I like how it's kind of weird, and also that they are spiritually connected to these animals."

"It's about capitalism."

"I don't think so."

"No, it's obviously an allegory for capitalism."

"I think it can be about that and about animal spirituality."

I can see the disappointment in his face again. I try to change the subject to Pride, but he becomes quiet. I stay quiet as well. The sound of traffic below is the only conversation between us. I think about the cars, and how the exhaust rises and becomes part of the air we breathe and the dark sticky coating around our lungs. He asks me if I had fun last night. I lie and say yes.

"What was your favourite part?

"I don't know, the music?"

"Why are you saying that as a question?"

"Because I don't really know. I can see everyone enjoying the music, and I'm sure it's good. I just don't think I'm having fun like everyone else. They all stay out late and get high and dance and I just am not good at those things."

"It's easy, just dance. Or maybe have some drinks!"

"But I try that. I can drink and drink, and I get more annoyed. The more drunk I am, the more I hate everything around me."

"That doesn't sound good."

"It feels fucking terrible. Then I get jealous. I look around and see everyone happy, and I feel so miserable that I don't know what that is. I can't be like you, no matter how hard I try. You love everything."

"I guess I do love everything ... and I love that about myself."

"I know. I really and honestly am happy for you, but I hate everything, and I hate that about myself." I kiss him and tell him that I have to leave. He frowns, but even his frown looks like a smile.

*

When I get home, I sit on the couch and try to run through a list of things I love. I love beer, but then again, consuming beer makes me sad or angry. My roommate walks out of her room.

"What are you doing?" she asks.

"Thinking about stuff I love."

"Ha, you hate everything. Wait, what about cake?"

"Nah, I fucking hate cake. Too sweet."

"Well, you lost me."

When she heads back into her room, something deep in my gut tells me that I need to bake pies, and not just one or two, but eight pies. I make a raspberry and rhubarb, a strawberry, and peach pies.

"I love pies!" I yell out.

My roommate comes out of her room and stares at my pie baking. She stares for a long time without saying anything.

"Why the fuck are you baking pies?"

"Because I like pie."

"But since when do you bake pies?"

"Now! I bake pies now. This is my new thing. I bake pies, and I give them out to people, because I love pie."

"This is weird."

"It's not weird. I love pies. I'm a pie person."

By the end of the evening I have baked all eight pies and cooled them off. I take a picture of them and post them online. It gets three likes and someone comments, "you bake pies?"

*

I meet with an ex for lunch. The patio is covered, the sound of cars splashing rain is only lightly dulled. The gas heater warms the space. Uncertain why I am doing this, I panic; small goosebumps rise on my arms. I am twenty minutes early to make sure I'm prepared for him. A cold sweat covers my face. I look up and down the street for him. He texts that he is going to be ten minutes late. I order a third beer and quickly guzzle it down. When he arrives, I pretend that I am checking my phone.

"Why are we meeting here?" he asks.

"I baked you a pie," I explain.

He stares at me in confusion. "Since when do you bake pies?"

"I bake pies now, okay? Why is that so surprising to people? I look like the type of guy who bakes pies, and I bake pies now. This is my thing."

"You know I'm dating someone now."

"Then share the fucking pie with him, I don't care."

"It's a pretty small pie. I'm not sure how we're going to share it."

"It's a nice gesture, okay? It's a nice thing I'm doing for you. Just say thank you."

"Are you drunk?"

"I don't know. Probably. Are you high right now?"

"A little bit."

We spend the rest of the meal talking about the first time we met. He reminds me of the time we had sex in the alleyway.

"Did you hear about Raymond?" he asks.

"No."

"He's doing porn now."

"That's so fucking tacky."

"I always forget how judgmental you are."

I go silent then excuse myself to go to the bathroom. In the bathroom, I can see the sweat covering my forehead. I remind myself, "You're okay." I wipe the sweat from my forehead and walk back to the table.

He brings the conversation back to our sexual encounters over the years and gets that glazed look in his eyes. The bill arrives, and the total comes to $69.69. He laughs at the number and tells our server that we were just talking about this time we were having sixty-nine. She gets uncomfortable and I head off to the bathroom again.

When I get back, he's got his keys in his hands and asks me to come back to his place. I pretend like I probably won't but then agree to a quick nightcap. When we get there, he pushes me onto his bed. I don't bother pretending to resist.

When we're finished, he rinses off in the bathroom. "You gotta go, though," he yells. "My boyfriend is coming back soon."

I nod and grab my clothes. He walks naked over to the pie and takes large bites out of it.

"Good pie, though, eh?"

*

He has my bike. He has my bike, and I need to figure out if I can be with someone as happy about the world as he is. I drive down to his apartment, and I bring along the pies I baked. *The first usage of "yum" dates back to the late nineteenth century. It wasn't popularized until mid-twentieth century. According to some research, the word emerged from the sound of smacking lips. This is debatable.*

He takes the pie and quietly eats it in front of the television. I slowly eat my pie as well, looking at him. I can't seem to finish mine; it tastes old, or like Styrofoam with a hint of jam. He's quiet and contemplative. He finishes the pie, puts the empty tin on the table, and walks to the kitchen.

"You didn't say if you enjoyed the pie or not," I say.

He slowly turns to me with a look of confusion and then a look of despair. "I. Loved. It." He makes sure to break in between each word. "It was honestly one of the most delicious pies I have ever tasted," he says, like he'd been drowning and that pie pulled him from the ocean.

I'm thinking about how the pie is already a day old, the crust already soggy at the base. Its flakiness turning to mush. "Oh," is all I can say.

"You sound disappointed."

"I just thought maybe you didn't like it, and you kind of love everything."

"I don't love everything."

"No, you kind of do."

"I hate stuff too!" he says cheerfully.

"No, you don't. That's sweet, but you really don't."

He rubs his hands on my back.

"I do! I hate racism."

"That doesn't count."

"I hate inequality!"

"Still not really something that counts."

"Oh, I really hate spinach! Well, only the weird feeling it gives your teeth after you eat it. But, you know what? When you cook it, that feeling isn't there. I do love cooked spinach."

I kiss him, and he pulls me in. He pulls my pants down, and I try to shut my mind off. He has me against the kitchen sink.

He looks up at me and smiles. "Oh, yum."

Hummus and bread. My genitals turn to hummus and bread, stale unimpressive hummus and bread. I close my eyes, but everything is hummus and bread. The sunset is hummus and bread, the wine and cheese are hummus and bread, the plants and the beautiful ocean are hummus and bread. The pies? The pies are just hummus and bread pies baked in tinfoil pans that will find themselves in a hummus and bread landfill that will clog up this hummus and bread earth.

"I can't do this," I blurt out. He looks disappointed but not surprised. "I'm just not a happy positive person, and I just can't do this."

"Why don't you try."

"I don't know. I just can't."

"I could make you happy."

"You really couldn't. And it would make me more miserable to watch you try."

He nodded in a way that said yes but really meant no.

The word "yum-o" was popularized by a television show starring Rachael Ray. The band Ohio Express had a hit song with the lyrics "yummy yummy yummy, I got love in my tummy." There is a theory that the sweetness of yams is potentially where the word came from. On Thanksgiving, yams are typically served. My ex used to bake me yams with marshmallows that I pretended to like. I would eat as little as possible to save room for pie. He was always very good at baking pie.

He looked at me. "What are you thinking about?"

"Pie."

"See, you love something. That's a start. What else?"

i was showing you where my friends were getting married, and you corrected me, said this was the hotel where we used to go for brunch. you drove the car in the wrong direction because the last time we drove up this hill, the car flipped over. this time, we were on a giant cliff and you kept trying to move the car, but we were stuck. the silver car was at the edge, just about to fall into the water, and we had to leave it there or else we might fall in. somehow time leapt ahead, and zio showed us where the car was now. it shrunk and was frozen on the water. when we got into the car, the ice it had settled on broke off, and we floated into the ocean.

CRAIG HAS VERY NICE SKIN

My skin is fitting weirdly on my body today. I woke up this morning, and it felt looser than usual. When I checked the mirror, I could see that there was extra skin drooping from my eyes, some folding around my butt, some gathered around my elbows.

I usually have someone fix this. It would be very embarrassing if my skin were just to fall off. When I was young, my skin was too tight, and everyone would notice. I would make up excuses like, "I have an eating disorder" or "I'm just too big for my body." Now my excuses are, "I'm too tired," and "I'm getting old." It's becoming harder and harder to keep my skin firmly covering my body. Taping my skin tight with duct tape only works under my clothes, and Botox only lasts so long before my skin begins to loosen all around my face.

Craig was coming over tonight, so I needed to figure out the best way to quickly tighten up my skin. I made several calls, but it was impossible to book an appointment. I decided to wear a hat that sat low on my head. I lined the hat with duct tape so that it would hold my forehead skin up.

Craig arrived early, which wasn't like him. He had also been drinking. He came very close to my face for a kiss and then stopped. "What's up with your forehead? You look surprised." I stared at him until he changed the subject.

Craig has very nice skin. His body is the same age as my human coverings, but his is perfect and fits tightly around all of his body.

"Let's go out." He grabbed my arm, but I pulled away.

"Why?" I asked.

"Because you need to go out more and meet men!"

I don't like meeting men. I especially don't like the bar. It's filled with people, and they can't manage their space. I have my space, and they have their space, but at the bar, everyone wants to share space. I can feel them groping at my skin, feeling it loosen. There is this way humans take up space, like water in buckets, or hair in sewage drains.

"Why?" I asked.

"We're not staying in again. I've already had a couple of drinks, and I'm not wasting them on watching more episodes of *The Blue Planet*."

I thought about sitting and watching *The Blue Planet* with Craig. He'd ask me to sit closer, maybe say that he didn't mind my loose skin. I would lay my head on his chest, and maybe a bit of my skin would fall off, but he wouldn't care. And maybe some of my skin would slide down, and he'd think to himself how sexy it would be if I took off all of my skin. He would slowly uncoil it, and my body could actually breathe. I could relax, let my fur and wings loosen.

Craig grabbed my jacket and pulled me out the door. A cab arrived promptly. It was missing a headlight and the left side of the car showed several scrapes. The drive of the cab was an older man.

I slipped into the front seat. "Your headlight is out. That's actually illegal," I said.

"Sir, you don't have to sit in the front seat," he responded.

"Also, you have scratches along the left side of your car. Is that from an accident or a bad parking job?"

"No, some guy hit me."

"How can they be from someone hitting you if they're long scratches? I would like you to drive safely please." The cab driver stopped responding to my questions for the duration of the drive. The drive took thirteen minutes. The car swerved, and I felt my body flail back and forth in the seat. He pulled up to the bar. "Here's your money. I'm not tipping you because I felt uncomfortable," I added. I could see Craig waiting in the car and passed him a few extra dollars.

When we entered the bar, the space was already filled with too many people. I decided to keep my jacket on in case we decided to leave early.

"Steve, you have to take your jacket off—you'll die of sweat in here."

"People don't die of sweat, they die of dehydration." Craig stared at me until I put my jacket in coat check.

Craig purchased me a drink. I sipped it slowly knowing how quickly I can become too intoxicated, but then I started taking larger gulps until the drink was just ice and a squeezed lemon.

Craig motioned for us to take a seat on the open plush couches. Immediately, several men stood in front of us, their bodies blocking the rest of the club from view.

I waved at them. "Hello, excuse me, you are rather close to us." The music was too loud. "Excuse me, you're getting rather close to us." The men's butts inched closer until they were directly in front of our faces. Craig seemed pleased by this.

"Look how tight those guy's jeans are!" Craig laughed. "They're so fucking tight I can see this guy's iPhone contact list."

"I'm going to go get us another drink." I excused myself.

As I walked from the couch to the bar, I squeezed between men whose hands coincidentally dropped to graze against my butt. I was thankful my jeans were sturdy enough to keep their hands from getting into my pants. The bartenders were shirtless, which meant it was after midnight. I ordered two more drinks, and they went down faster than the last.

I started to forget about my skin.

When I got back to Craig, there were several men surrounding him. I hesitated, but Craig noticed me and pulled me in. He began to introduce each one. "This is Kyle, he works in law. This is Jeffrey, he's a doctor from Seattle. And this is Kareem, he's a scientist, I think."

"Nice to meet you." I stared intently at the foreheads of each of the men. Their skin fit so perfectly on their faces. "You have very nice skin," I commented to one. I remembered my skin and quickly finished my drink.

Kyle looked at me. "So what do you do, Steve?"

"I'm an accountant," I said.

"Oh, do you like numbers?"

"No. But it's a good salary, and I'm very good at calculations." Kyle was staring at me. I was supposed to ask the next question. I noticed tattoos running down his bicep. They were thick lines interweaving. "I noticed your tattoo. Is that a fish?"

"No, it's more just a kind of abstract tribal tattoo."

"What does it mean?"

"I guess it doesn't really mean anything, more just a visual thing. Do you like it?"

"No—uh, I mean, no." I walked away then walked back over to him, "I'm sorry that I don't like your tattoos." I walked away. I walked back to him. "I mean that I don't like tattoos, not just your tattoos. I like your skin, though." I walked away.

Craig gave me a shot of tequila and another drink. I forgot about my skin. I was dancing.

Other people were dancing.

A man danced with me, pressed against me. "I like your hat," he said.

"Thank you. I purchased it at a store," I replied.

I had to go to the bathroom, so I excused myself. When I returned, the man was dancing with someone else. Craig pulled me into a conversation with the man from Seattle.

"Steve, we're trying to figure out if you're a bear."

"No, I'm not a bear."

"You're totally a bear."

"No, I assure you, I'm human like you."

Everyone started to laugh. I had either made a joke or they were laughing at me.

"Obviously, but, like, Jeffrey is a wolf, and I'm more of an otter cub, but you're a total bear."

"No. I'm not." I felt myself becoming bothered. "I'm quite obviously a human—look at my human skin!"

"Steve, you're hilarious. Weird, but totally fucking funny." Craig was drunk.

My skin. I focused on my breathing. I could feel my skin sliding. If I focused long enough on my breathing, my skin wouldn't fall off.

"Why am I so funny?" I responded.

"I dunno. You're just kind of weird. But, like, a good weird."

"I don't think I'm very funny or weird. I think maybe you are the funny and weird one."

My skin.

"Maybe that's why you constantly have to jump from man to man to man to feel some sort of belonging," I yelled. Craig stopped laughing.

Skin loosened.

"Maybe that's why you can't last in a relationship longer than a month."

And loosened.

"Maybe ..."

I could feel my skin start to slip off, but I couldn't stop it. "That's why everyone talks about you the way they do." My skin was a loose pair of pants being held together by a thick belt. "Maybe that's why you can't just stay home and watch *The Blue Planet* with me." My skin was so loose, I could feel it flapping around; my hat was the only thing holding it together. "Maybe if we just stayed home and watched *The Blue Planet* we could fall in love, and I wouldn't have to go to this place anymore." I felt my skin drop from my body.

"Dude, what's wrong with your skin?"

I ran quickly into the handicap bathroom stall and tried to fix my face. My skin was drooping so low. I remembered to breathe. Breathe in, breathe out. If I could calm down, I could get my skin back on just enough to quickly make it out of the club without anyone noticing. I looked in the mirror, and it started to look manageable. I lowered my hat over my face, covering my eyes.

For a moment, though, I thought about letting it just fall off altogether, walking out the bathroom door without it. Maybe everyone wouldn't notice. Or maybe they would all notice and then be amazed at how beautiful I look without my skin. Maybe one man would walk up to me and say, "I can't keep my eyes off you. Did you know that you're beautiful?" Maybe he would kiss me and hold me, tell me that skin was just a disgusting layer of flaking elastic bands covering beautiful flesh and fur. Maybe he would kiss my face, my chest, tell me that I was perfect with my flesh hanging out. I then imagined us walking out of the bar together and the men outside screaming at the sight of my body without skin.

I pressed the folds of my skin closer to my eyeballs. I walked out of the bar. I couldn't find Craig. He must have left with someone.

When I got home, I sat on the couch and turned on *The Blue Planet*. I watched as the birds dived and swooped and ate prey by gulping fish from cold blue water. I felt my wings itch. When the program ended, I went into my bathroom, pulled off my hat, took off my clothes, and stared into the mirror. After a moment, I pulled down the skin around my eyes and lifted it off my face. I pulled the skin down from my face to my chest. I pulled my skin down from my chest to my knees. I let the skin drop to the floor and stepped out of it.

I called Craig and apologized. I scooped my wings around my face to block the mirror.

DATE: THATDUDE

He walked into the lounge. Ryan checked his text messages. ThatDude would be in the back and wearing a fedora. Ryan noticed that he looked nothing like his profile picture. He quickly turned around and deleted ThatDude's number.

TROPICAL BILL MURRAY ISN'T YOUR BEST FRIEND

There was a lot of beer. You were drunk. You stole someone's smokes and burned through them in an hour.

By the time you were at the bar, you were already yelling at a few men. You asked them if you were adorable. They answered "yes." You responded, "Then tell everyone I'm adorable." No one found this adorable.

You turned to R, who was pointing at someone across the room. He was excited. You looked at where he was pointing and noticed a man in a Hawaiian shirt. His hair was white, thin, frizzy around his ears. Your friend lumbered toward you and whispered, "It's totally fucking Bill Murray, dude! But he's wearing a Hawaiian shirt, so I don't know, he's, like, Tropical Bill Murray."

I noticed him as well. You squinted; your contacts were dry. You moved on to talk to H. He was staring at a cluster of men wearing tank tops that framed their muscles. I interrupted you to ask if you had seen the guy who looked like Bill Murray. You stared at the cluster of muscle men.

"You should talk to them," I said.

"Yeah, and what am I going to say?" you asked.

"I dunno. 'Hey guys, I like your muscles. Does the attic match the basement?'" I laughed.

"That doesn't even make sense."

"It does, you just don't get it. But for real, go talk to them. That guy, what's wrong with that guy?" I pointed at a man across the room.

"His eyes look kind of close together."

"That guy?"

"He keeps talking with his eyes closed; that's really irritating."

"Okay, the one in the yellow tank top."

"He's definitely over thirty and wearing a yellow tank top."

I nodded in agreement and pushed through the crowd, pulling you with me.

"Where are you taking me?"

"To talk to the dude in the yellow tank top."

I introduced you quickly then ran off. You gave me the look of death. I smiled back.

Then I went to talk to Tropical Billy Murray. His smile made me feel at ease. When I squint hard enough, I notice that he's even a little bit handsome. Soft eyes make me feel safe, so I always fall in love with the tired and sad looking guys. He flips through his phone, and he's look at art. He's a painter, I think. I kind of don't remember this part, but yes, a painter. He has all of these realistic portraits of young men, and I ask if he will paint me. He shakes his head, laughs, and shows me his most recent work. It's all geometric shapes. When I blur my vision, I can see the earlier portraits he showed me.

R walked up to us and yelled, "Did you know you look like Bill Murray?"

I looked at R with that disappointed face that I do—you know the one. Tropical Bill Murray smiled that perfect Bill Murray smile and nodded. "Yes, I've been told that before."

R smiled for a long time, then walked away.

Tropical Bill Murray and I went through the rest of his photos, and I mumbled something about wanting to be Facebook friends or follow each other on Twitter. I can't remember.

Anyway, you were talking to tank-top guy, and I return to you to get into the conversation. You two were arguing about something. You were yelling, "But that's not even physically possible!" The conversation stopped when I arrived, so I tried to muster up a new conversation.

"So, I heard that Westboro Baptist Church guy died."

Everyone nodded.

"We should protest his funeral!" one guy yelled out.

"No, that's exactly what he would have wanted. We should just pretend that guy never existed," you said.

There was a silence, so I asked another question. "What does love mean to you?" I was being ironic, but the words stumbled out sincerely.

There was another silence, much longer this time.

"What's wrong with you?" you asked me.

"I don't know. I thought it was a good question."

"You're always so fucking intense."

You stormed off, and I stared at yellow tank top and asked him if he'd bought his shirt at Gap Kids. He called me a bitch and I nodded in agreement. I tried to break the tension by asking, "Did you ever hear about the time Bill Murray walked up to a guy, ate his french fry, and said, 'No one will ever believe you.'?"

Silence again so I went and ordered another beer.

Tropical Bill Murray was at the bar when I got there. He did card tricks, he was taking tequila shots off men's chests, he was high-fiving everyone in the room. He was telling us the stories about when he used to work in the circus, and about all the people he'd met in his life. He balanced three men on his shoulders, he danced on the tables. We held him over our shoulders chanting, "TBM-TBM-TBM!" I think. I can't really remember.

Then we went to another bar. We took off our shirts. Well, you took off your shirt, then you forced me to take off my shirt. I stole R's big basketball jersey and wore that for the rest of the night pretending it was a dress and asking random men if they would take me to the prom. There was A&W. There were onion rings. There was a French guy. I can't remember. There was the cab we both jumped into—or did someone else drive us home?

Somehow, the morning happened. I called you up and suggested brunch. You declined. I went anyway, sat at the bar, ate my eggs, drank several morning beers, and texted to ask you to go out for drinks. You declined. I headed out for drinks anyway and found R and C. When I texted you to say that we were at the bar, you replied, "on my way."

"Tropical Bill Murray!" You pointed at him. I quickly rushed to great him. He looked tired.

"Oh, hey, guys."

"Do you remember us?" I shouted with adoration.

"Of course. How are you two?"

"We're doing good—what about you?" My smile was so wide I looked like Pacman about to consume ghosts.

"I'm alright." He looked back and forth between us. "I need to go back to my friends now."

Tropical Bill Murray walked back to a handful of men with silver hair. They sipped their beers and looked into the glasses.

"What's wrong with Tropical Bill Murray?" I asked you.

You pointed at some guys across the room, said they might be nice to talk to.

"They're wearing cargo pants." I said.

"So what?"

"Who wears cargo pants?"

"I don't know. Cargo pants enthusiasts? Maybe someone who has a lot of things that need pockets? Maybe an explorer?"

"Dora doesn't wear cargo pants. At least she's smart enough to get a backpack."

"You're an asshole." You walked away.

I sobered up. We walked over to Lolita's for a late dinner. You started to joke about how I was going to be single forever. I joked too.

"You're picky. Didn't you break up with someone once because they kept saying 'epic'?"

"So what! You broke up with a guy because he didn't eat sushi."

"What about the guy who was too nice?"

"Ugh, that guy. He was so nice, like, go save a fucking orphanage while you build a hospital that creates oxygen," I laughed.

"You're fucking terrible."

I nodded. "I know, but it's always like this: you meet a guy and you like him, so you go through all of his Facebook photos and think about how handsome he is. Then, after a couple of weeks, you start to notice all of the bad photos. You focus on those, and soon those are the only photos you can see. You slowly stop texting him, and it all kinda goes to shit after that."

You looked at me with that fucking look I can't stand, the one that says I have it all wrong. "You have to start at the end, dumbass."

"Fuck off."

"No. Listen. Start at the point where all of the photos he has are bad. Start there."

"Okay, Gandhi."

"You can't always joke everything away."

No one talked for a bit. Everyone checked their phones.

"I'm bored. Let's order shots."

That night I went through a list of all of my ex-boyfriends. There was the guy who smoked too much pot, the one in the failed band, the Quebec guy, the one who stole from me, the one who would never let us be seen in public, the one who only wanted to be seen in public. I tried to imagine them as tank tops. Then as different versions of Bill Murray. Then each of them wearing different Hawaiian shirts. "You're not Tropical Bill Murray," I said to each of them as they put on their Hawaiian shirts. "Tropical Bill Murray isn't even real."

When I finally passed out, I had a fever dream:

Tropical Bill Murray is sitting alone at the bar. I sit with him, and instead of speaking, words fly out of his mouth in physical form. I try to organize them in order to understand him. He has a secret he must tell me, and once I have the words in order I can know the secret. "I'm sorry," I keep telling him. There are too many words, and I can't figure out what goes where. The words are pouring onto the floor, and I drown.

I woke up, my bed soaked. I went to get a glass of water and saw that you were still on my couch. You were looking out at the grey Vancouver sky from my window. You looked at me and said, "Tropical Bill Murray would wear cargo pants."

"I heard once that Bill Murray crashed a bachelor party and hung out with those guys all night," I replied.

"I heard that he attended this random kid's ice cream party."

"I heard that one time, Bill Murray joined in on a couple's engagement photos."

"What if it was Bill Murray?"

"It's not," I said.

I could hear the wind pressing against the window.

"You ran out of hope."

"To be honest, I never liked Bill Murray in the first place. I heard he's not that great of a guy."

DATE: SMALLTOWNBOY

Ho.

I hope you meant hi.

:p

TONGUE-OUT SMILEY FACE

;p

What does that mean?

I dunno, like ;p I dunno

Uh?

It's like, I said something and it's
weird so ;p

Well I don't know what the fuck to
do with that.

///

We had been travelling down the road for a couple of hours. Long past any city, just mountains and smoke from forest fires enveloping the sky. He finally pulled off a ramp for a stop at Dairy Queen. I let my arm hang out the window.

"You want anything?" he asked.

"No." I pulled my arm from the window and into my lap. "Maybe an Oreo Blizzard."

He parked the car, zipped up his pants, and let out a fart before getting out of the car.

"Thanks, because you couldn't have waited until you left the car."

"Whatever, my farts don't even smell."

"The worst part is that you believe that."

///

Therapist sat back, smiled, and waited for the conversation to start. It took a few minutes before she gave up and began asking questions. "So, why are you here?"

"Um, I guess because I feel weird, or I don't know if I feel anything, honestly."

"Well, that's something."

"I don't really get how this works."

"What do you want out of this?"

"I guess ... not to feel weird or something."

"Okay, I guess that's a start. Maybe we can talk about what feeling 'weird' is to you. Are you with someone, are you single?"

"I think I'm with someone."

///

He came back to the car and passed the Oreo Blizzard over to me. I began to swirl it around, attempting to find the spaces where mostly vanilla was. We drove out of the small town of Princeton on the way to Kelowna. I slipped in a few naps during the ride.

When we pulled up to the ranch, there were already several people drunkenly swerving around the house. He giggled and passed me his phone. There were several photos of me sleeping with my mouth open and him putting things in it.

I laughed, punched him, then got out of the truck. My brother was puking into a bush while his girlfriend screamed at him. You could tell she was just as drunk as he, but her version of vomit came out in the form of verbal abuse. We walked up to them, and she continued to berate him without hesitation. "You're a fucking fat drunk asshole," she said, "you drunk, fat asshole. Hey, guys. Get off the fucking ground and get to our tent, you dirt bag."

She waved us off as she pulled him out of the bush that was now covered in his puke.

///

I woke up and reached to the nightstand to grab my glasses. They weren't there, but I kept reaching over until I felt something soft and warm. I kept my eyes closed, knowing what this familiar softness was.

"Can I have my glasses back?"

He lowered his voice. "First, you must give professor penis a kiss."

I rolled over to see my glasses placed on top of his penis, with his pubic hairs parted to the side. I tried not to laugh.

"Well, it is the head you think with; it might as well have glasses and a doctorate."

"Give professor penis a kiss."

I grabbed my glasses swiftly, hitting him harder then expected. He dropped to the ground, laughing in pain.

///

Can I come over?

:p

Is that a yes or a no?

///

When I arrived home, he was lying on his belly, eating Nutella, and watching *Yo Gabba Gabba*. He was high again.

"How was work?"

"I was fired."

"Oh ..."

He turned off the TV and turned around. He had been crying.

"Didn't know *Yo Gabba Gabba* was such a dramatic show."

He set aside the Nutella and rubbed his hands together awkwardly. "Can we talk?"

"You have got to be fucking kidding me."

He sat there with his eyes watering, which quickly turned into heaving fits of tears. "I just don't feel the same way anymore."

"Oh, you have feelings now, you fucking asshole."

"See, you turn into a bitch every time I try to talk."

"Stop crying. Stop fucking crying. You don't get to cry and break up with me, that's not how this works."

"I'm sorry." His crying became uncontrollable.

"I'm supposed to be crying. Stop crying. Stop it!"

We sat in silence for several minutes. He continued to sob. He finally looked up and stared at me with moisture outlining his eyes.

"How come you never cry?"

"Because I'm not sad, asshole. I'm mad."

"I'm worried you don't feel anything except anger."

"You think that everyone has to fucking feel everything? Look at you. You can't even watch a children's show and you're looking at me like I'm a monster? You just broke up with me!"

"Do you even like me?"

"Sure! Of course I do."

"No, but like, do you actually like me? Tell me something you like about me."

I couldn't come up with anything. There was something. My mind went blank. I grabbed my stuff and walked out of the door. He yelled something about picking up his stuff tomorrow. I threw him the middle finger—"Feel this."

///

We set up our tent near the water. The creek slowly streamed past us. A slight breeze passed under my shirt, and I hugged my arms against myself to keep warm. He pulled me in and covered my body with his, protecting me from the cold. He was twice my size. Sometimes I felt like I could hide under him. Sometimes it felt like the weight of his body would push my shoulders into the ground.

We grabbed our cooler full of beer and whiskey and headed toward the bonfire. The party was in full swing. We took shots of whiskey to catch up.

I stood next to the bonfire. My brother was asleep on his girlfriend's lap. I pulled out a beer and stared into the fire. In the corner of my eye, I thought I saw a man in deep red flannel, far back in the forest. I looked up and he was gone.

My boyfriend was already three beers in when he came to the bonfire. He had shotgunned two in just a few minutes. His eyes were glazed, and he began to grind up against my body. "You're funny," he slurred.

He pulled off his shirt to show me a scratch from drunkenly climbing the rocks, then he pulled down his nipples. "Look how angry my nipples are! Angry nipples," he mumbled. "Kinda looks like you."

///

Sometime I close my eyes and I can turn into wallpaper. I hold his hands, and it feels like an ocean is splitting our bodies. I think about what it would be like to let go.

///

When I got to his apartment, he was on his belly watching *Dora the Explorer*. He was high again.

"Fuck, I wish I had a magical backpack and, like, a map that told me where to go."

"You have an iPhone. You literally have a map that tells you where to go."

"Why do you always have to shit on everything?"

///

It was too dark to see, and I had lost the flashlight. I was soaking wet from the downpour. I could feel a familiar salivation in my mouth. My throat felt metallic, but my stomach felt like acid was swirling around with chunks of processed beef. Thinking about the burgers we ate didn't help.

I began to spit excessively, trying to get my mouth to stop salivating. It became too much, so I ran to the sound of the river and threw up over and over again. I felt the cold stones between my fingers. As I spat out the remnants of vomit, I could hear them gently splash into the water. I lay down and put my head into the freezing creek.

I could see a light bouncing down the hill toward me, shining in my direction. It looked like there was a small town in the middle of the forest. I blinked and it was gone. I felt someone's hand slip under my body and lift me up just as I blacked out.

///

He called me later that night, apologized, and asked if we could work things out. I paused for a moment and said, "Sure."

"Can you come over?" he asked.

I showered, grabbed some clothes, and headed over to his place.

When I arrived, he was already in bed, pitching a tent and giggling. He reached from the bed, pulled me in. "You want to role play?"

I tried not to laugh. He reached under my armpit and I collapsed. He knew I couldn't stand being tickled. After that, it was moments before my clothes were ripped off and we were having what he referred to as "porn star sex," aggressive thrusting for a camera that doesn't exist.

"Oh, there's this move I wanted to try. I saw it in a porn last night." He lifted my body and placed me on my head so that my neck was crunched.

"This isn't very comfortable," I gurgled through clenched teeth.

He finished, rolled over, and began to make fake snoring sounds. Bursting into laughter, he pulled me in and tightened his grip into a suffocating cuddle.

"Okay, you get three minutes of cuddle action."

I leaned into him.

"Ugh, you're like an oven." He rolled over.

///

When I woke in the morning, he was already off to work. I pulled on my shorts and shuffled into the kitchen to make coffee. I looked around to find my Post-it notes everywhere, most of which had cute things written on them like, "for my babe" or "one coupon for snuggles." But the rest had "do not touch" and "can you please take your stuff home next time."

///

We packed up our tent. The ranch was quiet and covered in dew. My parents sat on the patio sipping from mugs. We sat down, and they poured us coffee.

My parents began to complain about the neighbours, Sally and Mark. They had a very impressive garden and more dogs than any family should have. My parents were certain that Sally and Mark had trained the dogs to shit only in my parents' yard so that they had to clean the dog poop and the neighbours' garden would be untouched. I stopped paying attention to their ramblings when my mother interrupted my thoughts. "Are you still taking your anti-depressants?"

"Mom, I never took anti-depressants," I replied.

"Oh. Weird. I don't know why I thought that."

We slipped past my brother, who was passed out on a lawn chair. After a quick breakfast at the diner in town, we drove back toward Vancouver. We didn't talk much. He mumbled, "I guess this means I'm not getting any road head."

///

"You can't shut down every question I ask you."

"I just don't know how to answer these questions. I don't know."

"Well, you came to me for therapy, so you have two options: you can either start looking for answers or disappear."

///

The first time he broke up with me, I called an ex-boyfriend to come over. This is what I did after every breakup. I would call my previous boyfriends, have sex with them, then beg them to leave immediately afterward. Daisy chaining. That's what my therapist called it. As if I was in some unstoppable loop, chaining one ex to the next, looping in and out, back and forth, some loops much stronger than others.

///

"I'm worried I don't feel anything."

Therapist nodded.

///

We checked into the motel, quickly took a shower, and got into bed. He looked at me with that look which meant he was either about to fart or to say something that would hurt me. "Can you sleep in the other bed tonight?" I stared at him for about a minute without saying anything, kissed him, and jumped into the second bed. He flicked on the TV and we watched *Clueless* until we fell asleep.

I woke up to the sound of scratching. I looked over and saw him sitting in front of the mirror with his head down.

"Are you okay?"

He didn't respond. I felt dizzy. "Are you okay?" I shook my head to clear the dizziness, but he got up and walked toward the door.

"Please don't go," I yelled. He opened the door, turned around, and looked directly at me. When his eyes finally locked onto mine, his body lifted and he floated up into the clouds.

I was screaming when he finally hit me in the head with a sock. "Would you shut the fuck up! I'm trying to sleep." I'd been hallucinating again.

I threw the sock back at him. "I was having another nightmare, asshole." I left the motel room. It was very late and we were in the middle of nowhere, so there wouldn't be any place open to go to. I walked for a while, going further into the forested area than I should have. I saw a light flickering, and I could hear music. It was coming from a small pub in the middle of the forest. There were only a couple of people inside. I walked up to the bar and sat next to a man who was fiddling with his phone. He had on that deep red flannel shirt I had seen the night before. Just underneath his hands was a small daisy chain.

"Did you make that?" I asked.

"No," he smiled. "Someone made it for me. How did you get here?"

"I don't know."

"Well, that's usually how it happens."

His body was twice the size of mine. He ordered me a beer. It felt as if one sip was all it took for me to finish it.

"You were at the party. I noticed you before," I said.

"Yeah, that party wasn't for me. I'm local to this place. Too many city people coming in makes me feel uncomfortable."

"Sorry about that."

"Not you," he chuckled, "you're fine. Was that your boyfriend with you?"

"Um, kind of. I'm not sure what we are. I guess."

"Oh, okay."

Another beer arrived as soon as I was finished. Another arrived after I finished the second. He had a deep laugh and his eyes looked like charcoal. The beer went down fast, but my body felt light. I wasn't drunk, but my head felt loose.

He set his hand on my thigh and whispered, "I can give you anything you want."

I felt like I was floating. We walked over to a small cabin nearby. When he turned on the lights, there were small collector's toys everywhere, tiny plastic dolls from every cartoon I could recall. They covered every free surface. A tiny Dora the Explorer looked down from on top of the television.

He told me to grab us some beers from the refrigerator. I accidentally opened the freezer and noticed Oreo Blizzards lining the back wall. I shut the freezer, opened the refrigerator, and found cold crisp beers perfectly filling the entire interior.

"Why do you have so many old Blizzards?"

He laughed. "I never finish them, but I always feel bad throwing them out."

When I turned around, he was wearing nothing but his underwear. He pulled me toward the small bed that sat right in the middle of where a living room should have been. Itchy wool sheets covered the bed. It took him no effort to lift me, and then he gently laid me down.

"I can give you anything you want," he whispered again into my ear. I felt his hands slip away from my back. My body floated above the bed. The lights began to bounce around the room.

"I want this." I pulled his hands toward my neck. Just as his hands clasped my throat, I disappeared.

///

"I was thinking about the tongue-out smiley face, and I thought of you."

you came back to life. you looked the same and talked the same, but something felt wrong. it wasn't until i was driving out of an underground garage that I realized it would be impossible for you to come back. your body has been decomposing in the earth for over two years. you said that as long as you took three pills a day your body would stay together. my landlord was telling me that it would be impossible for you to be alive. i asked you to tell me what you used to make me for dinner every time I played soccer. you said pizza, and i knew it wasn't you. you would remember the time i ate pizza and vomited throughout the night, which was why i wouldn't eat pizza until i was eighteen. you would remember this.

SEX DATE

1.

Therapist rested her head on her hand, smiled, and said, "You know, I think you're done talking about this guy." Therapist was determined, so I stopped. Therapist said it wasn't about him. Therapist reapplied her lip gloss, placed her hands on her lap, and asked me about work.

Earlier in the day, I'd had an interview for a new job. Therapist said my job was making me upset so I applied for new ones during my work breaks. Therapist asked me some questions to prepare me for the interview, like, "When was the last time you think you failed yourself?"

I recalled being in grade eight, attempting to perform in a talent show when I panicked, forgot all of the words, and then began to dance off stage. Just then, one of the older guys yelled out, "faggot." Therapist was upset that I wasn't taking this seriously. I told her that I always feel like I'm failing myself.

Later that night, I went for drinks with Ryan. Ryan is smart and financially successful. He's also generally attractive so he doesn't worry about being smart and pretends that he isn't.

Ryan asked me how my "slut summer" was going. We'd agreed that I needed to expand my sexual activities; Ryan had said it wasn't normal to have sex with just one person in your life. I'd agreed but told him I wasn't cut out for this slut business. I almost set up a date with a guy, but then I cancelled after finding out he was a principal at an elementary school.

"What's wrong with a principal?" Ryan asked.

I told him that when I imagined the sex, I was worried that I would think about his elementary school students and that made me uncomfortable.

"Gross," Ryan replied.

I wasn't explaining myself well. Therapist says that I do that sometimes.

Ryan looked frustrated and said, "If you don't want to know you're fucking a principal, stop asking them what their job is."

"I can't help it," I replied. "The conversations go from, 'hey' and 'sup' to 'top or bottom' and then I think, well, what if this guy works for McDonald's, and then I'm sucking the dick of some guy who spends his days greasing his forehead with chicken nuggets?"

Ryan laughed really hard for a moment then corrected me. "That's classist—and you love chicken nuggets. What you need to do is just go for it. Just set it up, no questions, and let your freak flag fly, girl."

It made me uncomfortable every time Ryan called me "girl." Therapist said it's because I have internalized homophobia, but I tried to explain that it was the word they used to call me before fists would come at me and my mind would go black. I told Ryan I didn't love chicken nuggets.

Later, when we were walking down the street, Ryan pointed at a man and said that he had a hot body. I asked if he knew that he was a homeless man, but Ryan said that he still had a hot body.

"Yeah, but from doing too many drugs," I replied. He said I was being classist again, and then said, "Where do you think those guys with giant muscles get their bodies? Drugs." I nodded in agreement. Therapist told me that my body dysmorphia is normal and common among gay men.

2.

"What do you like to do for fun?" I said frantically, trying to cover over my disappointment. He was not a very attractive man, and the picture on his profile used shadowing and was cropped in close to make him appear to be something else. I wondered whether people knew exactly what they looked like. I wondered if I think I look one way, but everyone else sees another me.

"You mean sexually?" he smiled.

"No, I meant for fun, like, in public."

"Oh, regular stuff, I guess."

"I like to knit. I know that doesn't sound exciting, but my mind tends to go into overdrive and so when I think about something that makes me think about something else and then something else and soon it's five in the morning, and I can't remember where I started. One time I didn't sleep for almost two days."

We stared at each other for a moment. He tried to sip from his coffee cup but realized it was empty. I attempted to change the conversation. "What do you get up to on your days off?"

"Sexually?" He smiled again.

"I meant not sexually."

"Oh ... I don't know, hang out with friends." He rolled his cup around on its edge in a circular motion. "I guess ... I like reading books."

I started to sweat. I was still wearing my coat, but I didn't want to take it off. I began to wipe the sweat from my forehead in case he noticed.

"Uh ... what do you do for work?" I asked

"I work for a bank. It's not really fun, but it pays the bills."

The sweat from my forehead became unmanageable. The more I sopped it up, the more he would notice. Therapist made a joke once that my anxiety must be great for my skin. I said to the guy, "I have to rush off. I forgot that I have to meet with a friend in a few minutes."

He offered to walk me back to my place. I agreed, since his place was along the way.

"So, like, what kind of sexual stuff are you into?"

"I'm pretty conservative," I said. "I don't really like to talk about it."

"Nice, we'll save that for tonight."

He gave me a hug and kissed me on the cheek. I told him I was at my block, then ran seven blocks in the opposite direction, deleting his number along the way.

3.

He walked up to me, handsome and smiling, and introduced himself. He had a thick European accent; I couldn't quite place it.

"Let's go for a walk." He placed his hand gently on my back and we began to walk toward the east side of town. It was late summer so I wore a

T-shirt and shorts. I had a few drinks beforehand so I was still warm from the alcohol.

We talked about our jobs. He was becoming a lawyer, or a city planner. I wasn't really paying attention; I was focusing on how I would explain my career.

I stood there quietly for ten minutes until he told me that he had better head off; he had plans.

4.

Ryan uses Botox. Ryan is twenty-nine. When we were sitting at the coffee shop, I asked him why, and he said it was to keep his face smooth. I said he was too young to be using Botox, but he said he was already getting wrinkles. I am twenty-seven.

We stepped out of the Blenz coffee shop. Ryan sipped his hot coffee through a straw and recounted the dates he'd had that week. Ryan goes on a lot of dates. I do not go on a lot of dates. My therapist says that I should try and go on more. Ryan's descriptions of his dates were paired with a list of deformities: Too fat, too old, hairline receding faster than his interest in the conversation, too ethnic, too rich, too poor, too boring, too caring, not caring enough, too lazy, too gay, not gay enough.

Ryan asked me about my week, and I told him about work. Work is boring. Ryan agrees. This week I Googled my name every day, but there's this other guy with my name, and he's much more successful than I am. Ryan tells me I have to stop Googling myself because nothing will come up. I know he's right, but I will keep Googling myself.

We rushed off to Numbers to get out of the rain. Ryan ordered a pitcher and a couple of shots. The bartender was dancing to the remix of a Cher song. There were only two people in the bar, and they were sitting alone at opposite ends of the pub. Ryan pulled out his phone and began to type.

"You know," he said, "what you need to do is set yourself up with some sexy photos on your Grindr account. Look at your profile. You can't wear a hat in your photo!"

I told him that I liked my photo. Ryan stared blankly at me and sipped his beer. He said I looked like a fag in that photo. I corrected him and said that was homophobic, and Ryan agreed.

5.

I pulled up to his place, got out of my car, and headed toward his door. He opened it before I could knock. He looked out from side to side and fist-punched my hand as I went in for the handshake.

When we sat on his couch, I sat too far away from him. He looked at me awkwardly so I asked him questions about his life. We talked about hookups, and he mentioned he kind of hated them. I agreed. We talked about long-term relationships and brought up our ex-boyfriends. He started to get worked up and emotional. I went to touch his knee as a sign of comfort, but I was sitting so far away from him that I had to lie on the couch to reach him. His knee jerked in response and he thanked me for a good night.

I walked back to my car and drove home.

6.

I slid under his arm, and he pulled me in, making sure that a pillow was tucked neatly under my head. My head was warm. I looked up at him and felt safe. I normally don't feel safe. I noted to myself to remember that I felt safe. He giggled and said he wanted this to last forever. He talked about work, the weather, his underwear being uncomfortable. I talked about work, the weather, my underwear never bothering me.

I told him about the sensitivity seminar we had at work about racism. After the seminar, I went online and noticed all of the racist comments from friends, even deleted a couple of my own comments. When I finished talking about the seminar, he pulled me in for a kiss. I said that some racism is so ingrained some people don't even notice it. He asked for examples.

"Like when people say all Asians are bad drivers," I said. And he nodded in agreement and said, "They really are bad drivers."

I told him I was tired. I waited until he fell asleep, grabbed my clothes, and left. I didn't feel safe.

7.

I triple-checked the address in my phone. Buzzer 308, I repeated to myself. I pressed the buzzer, waiting for him to ask who it was, but he just buzzed me in.

He was much shorter than he'd said and had a weird tattoo on his left arm that looked like a mix between a wizard's wand and a melted chocolate bar. The four glasses of wine I drank before the date kept me from running away. Therapist says I have a tendency to run away. He smirked, and I rushed toward him. My mouth smashed his face and our teeth clanged.

"You're an eager one."

I didn't respond. I was thinking of anything but this. Mostly about the laundry I could be doing. I had a load of whites in the washer, and I didn't want to put them in the dryer before I'd left because I was afraid the house could burn down unless I was there. So they were just sitting in the washer, and they get that weird smell when they're left in there too long. When I refocused, he had already removed all of my clothes. He undressed himself to reveal several more tattoos—a few Asian characters, some tribal tattoos, and something that looked like Tinkerbell. It was probably Tinkerbell. He was not Asian. Some people would assume he was a good driver because he wasn't Asian, but that's not true, that's racist. I never liked Tinkerbell. She was so small; it always seemed as though someone could crush her in their palm. I didn't like most Disney films. Some adults still go to Disneyland. Therapist says we hold onto our childhoods sometimes.

"You like when I hold your hands down like this?"

"I guess," I said. He held down my hands as he began to lick my face. He began to grunt. I began to laugh. Therapist says I laugh when I'm uncomfortable. The laughter stopped when I felt a series of sharp pains.

"Do you like when I pull your balls?"

"It kinda hurts," I replied.

"But, like, a good hurts?"

"Is there such a thing as good hurt?"

He stopped and looked at me. "Are you even enjoying this?"

"Yeah. Sure, it's fun." I wasn't sure if it was fun. Ryan always says that it's better to just agree during sex even if it's not fun.

He smirked again. "Yeah, this is kind of fun, isn't it?"

I thought about laundry again and all of the things I would miss if my apartment burned down.

8.

I met him at the beach, like he requested. He showed up in sunglasses and didn't take them off even after sunset. He pulled out beers from his bag, and we drank them quickly. I asked if he had cups to put them in but he laughed. He asked me to come home with him. He was handsome, so I said yes.

His place was dirty and smelled like garbage. When we sat down, he quickly leaned in for a kiss. We made out for a while until he stopped and asked if it was okay if he smoked some weed. I said okay. He asked if I wanted any, and I said, "No, I get paranoid and sleepy, and it makes my heart feel like it's going to beat out of my chest."

He smoked the weed then kissed me again. He asked if he could do some coke before we continued. I said okay. He asked me if I wanted some, and I said no. I tried coke once because Ryan said it would make me feel better, and then he had to rub my back as I breathed into a paper bag.

He inhaled the powder and kissed me again. Then he asked if we could just cuddle instead. I said okay. We got into his bed fully clothed and he held me, then held onto me for what felt like an hour before he fell asleep. I got up and left him in bed. When I was grabbing my jacket from his living room, I noticed all of the framed photos—there must have been about forty—of him with another man. There was a cold breeze from an open window that told me to leave. On the way home, I had chicken nuggets and wondered if Ryan was right, that I was classist.

9.

I met him at the corner, and he asked if we could walk toward the ocean. We walked for a couple of hours around the Seawall, and he told me everything he could think of: He told me about his childhood, he told me about his first dog. When he said we should head back to his place to get more comfortable, I held back for a moment and watched him walk forward. I waited for him to notice that I was gone and turn back, but he kept walking. He walked until he was out of sight. I never saw or heard from him again.

DATE: TOMMAS12

Ryan was finishing prepping the dinner for Tommas12. When the doorbell rang, Ryan felt a weird twinge in his chest. He shook it off and welcomed his guest in.

Ryan poured red wine for them, and they chatted on the couch. Blank is friends with blank, and I know blank from the gym who knows blank because he works at the bar. Ryan gulped the last of his wine to calm his nerves. His skin was tingling.

"Tom, should we open another bottle?"

"Charlie, actually. Tommas is my last name. Don't worry, I get that all the time." Charlie leaned in and kissed Ryan, awkwardly missing his lips. "Sorry, I'm actually blind in one eye so I don't have proper depth perception."

Ryan was about to make fun of him, but his skin turned hot.

"I'm kidding." Charlie leaned in and kissed Ryan.

The second bottle of wine came out, and Ryan could feel his nerves calm down.

"Can I be really honest? I actually really hate your profile on Grindr."

"Why?" Ryan laughed.

"Well, you write about what you don't want on your profile, and it comes across as really bitchy. Also, 'hiking buddy'? Really?"

"To be really honest, I fucking hate hiking," admitted Ryan. He laughed and felt his muscles clench. The light was too bright. He went to turn it down.

"Getting romantic already?"

Ryan laughed nervously. "Sorry, I just have light sensitivity sometimes."

"Sorry, I didn't know." Charlie reached out and touched Ryan's hand. Ryan felt his chest tighten further. He pulled away and went to the kitchen to put out the dinner. Charlie moved to the dinner table. They ate quietly, Charlie closing his eyes every time he put a morsel of food in his mouth.

"You're a really good cook!"

"Thanks, I've always liked cooking. Kind of wish I went to culinary school."

"You should!"

"Well, I did once, but I dropped out."

"Why?"

"I just didn't like it, I guess."

Charlie continued to eat until his plate was clear. When he finished his wine, he looked at Ryan. "Can I tell you something? This is actually the first time I've agreed to go on a date with someone I hooked up with." Ryan cleared the plates and brought over another bottle of wine. Charlie moved back to the couch. Ryan sat next to him, and Charlie moved in closer. He wrapped his arms around Ryan and kissed his neck, saying "This feels nice."

Ryan felt the room move. His chest tightened quickly and he felt dizzy. He tried to breathe, but the dizziness had set in too fast to breathe away. His skin was heating up.

"I have to go to the bathroom." Ryan stumbled to the washroom, locked the door, and lay down on the cold tile floor. He pulled his phone from his pocket and dialled her number.

A polite and quiet voice answered. "Ryan?"

"I ... I," Ryan stammered, lying flat on the floor.

"It's okay. Breathe slowly. Think of something to calm you down. Remember the summer in Banff?"

Ryan coughed in acknowledgement.

She continued, "When Dad was keeping nickel candies in his drawer? We always stole the candies just moments after he hid them, and he would always wonder where they went."

"He ... he thought it was Mom. How's Mom?"

"She's good."

Ryan unclenched his fist from his chest. "I need to call you back. I have a date over." Ryan pressed end on the phone. He got up, flushed the toilet, and washed his hands. He walked back into the living room. Charlie was looking at his books. "You okay?"

Ryan nodded. "I am just really tired. You should probably go." Charlie gave Ryan a gentle hug, said that they should do this again, and kissed him. Ryan's skin began to vibrate. When he left, Ryan went back to the bathroom and felt the cold tile floor cooling his skin.

Ryan texted "Hey, come over."

MuscGuy responded, "Get into bed, leave your door unlocked."

THE LICENSE

He sat back and rustled his shirt in annoyance. He was not supposed to be here, and he was going to do everything in his power to make it known. A group of young men and one young woman sat around the room. He would go in and out of listening to their stories. One of them had been going to a party and was pulled over for swerving too much; one had been getting off work late, was too drunk, and hit a pole; one was off to a club and went through a road block; one ran a red light and severely injured a family.

His son pulled up in front of the building. He fumbled with the door handle then immediately complained, "I have a couple drinks and then I am a drunk. Who say that? Who say I'm a drunk? When I was your age, I had a coupla drinks, then I go home. No one bug me. In Italy, everybody drunk and then they drive home. And no one say a thing. I remember, it was maybe forty years ago, we would go have a few drinks and then you head home. You remember that? That's when Elvis died. I bet he drive and drink. Remember when Elvis died?"

"Dad, I was born in 1985."

"Yeah, I guess you too young to remember."

The car pulled up to his house. He awkwardly fumbled out of the car. Once inside, he put on a small saucepan for the pasta. He ate dinner quietly in front of the TV. Cleaned his dishes. Turned off the TV.

///

He rushed over his words as the rest of the younger kids in the group looked at him. "I dunno why I'm here. I had a coupla beers and then they take my license and tell me I can no drive. I don't know. You have a bit of wine, and then you go play at the casino and have a few beers. The government, boy, they all crooks. Just want my money. In Italy, I could drink and then drive everywhere. Here, you drive a coupla blocks and you in jail. Not like you kids, you too young. You don't get it." He fiddled with his shirt, pushing against his thumb, the muscles of which had been tightening making it impossible for him to open his hand fully. Age, closing his fist. "And we gotta work. Well, I don't anymore, but these kids, they gotta work. I dunno." He fixated on his thumb. "I dunno."

His son arrived late today. "Boy, you make me wait out here in the freezing cold."

"Dad, it's summer."

"This place, it's always cold. Never gets hot. I dunno why she made us come here. Always raining and always cold. I can't walk anywhere. Then I walk, and I get sweaty so I gotta hold my jacket and then I get inside and they got that air conditioning and I getta cold again. Everyone here is crazy. You hear me?"

"Yes, Dad. Everyone is crazy. I got it."

"You no believe me. You always think you so smart."

"Yes, Dad. I am so smart."

"You just like you mother, think you so smart."

The car pulled up to his house. He fumbled out of the car. Inside, he put on a small saucepan for the pasta. He ate dinner quietly in front of the TV. Cleaned his dishes. Turned off the TV.

///

"So, I have a coupla drinks. And they say I'm too drunk. I was no drunk. No, I had a coupla beers, that's all. Just a coupla beers. And they sneak around the corner and tell me I'm a drunk. No! They drunk. They must be drunk. They take my breath and no let me see, so I say, no, I'm a no drunk. You drunk! And they take my license away. Now, I gotta sit here and talk to you stupid kids. You kids need to get a real job and then, then you can have a couple beers and drive. And I gotta drive her to the hospital, and I couldn't no do that anymore. And you take my license away. How was I supposed to drive her to the hospital? And she too sick to—"

He pulled at his thumb.

"I dunno, boy. I dunno where I am."

His son was waiting for him outside. "You come too early, you waste you time coming this early. You know, these stupid people. They don't understand. I need my license, I can no have you drive me everywhere. I gotta go work. I gotta get out of the house. I'm just supposed to sit and watch TV all day? I go crazy."

"Dad, you're retired."

"I know that. You don't think I know that? She leave us with all this debt. I don't know what she was thinking. She come into my life and she want a business and she want all those clothes and that car. She want all this diamonds and gold, and I can no afford that. And the casino. She just put money into that machine, into that god damn building. And now ... It don't matter."

He pulled out his wallet to give his son some money for the gas. A small key fell out of the wallet.

"Dad, what's this key for? It's almost rusted over."

"It no matter. For my truck."

"But your truck is broken."

"I just forgot about it. My truck was broken one time, and your mom, she got a key fixed for me. So the key work, but it didn't start the engine. It just get me into the truck. But later, I lose the key, and then I find it again. I found it in her purse. So I took it."

"We can get you a replacement."

"I'm not stupid. I know we can get a replacement. Everything break, though. Everything. You know it's that stupid curse."

"Dad, what?"

"That gypsy, I tell you about her, remember?"

"You have never told me this story before."

"Yes I did, you never listen. Before I get here, on the boat, in Italy. I pissed some woman off and she curse me. Why you think I get sick all the time?"

"I've never even seen you with a cold before."

"No, sick, like my head hurts sick. You get it too. You know, why we can no drink coffee. Sick, like head too fast sick."

"Dad, that's not a real thing. You weren't cursed."

"Yeah, I get cursed and all this bad things happen. I even tried to get rid of it, I go to that psychic and she broke an egg over my head and it turned black, or no, the egg inside was black."

"The yoke?"

"Yes! And she say she fixed it, but I still get sick and all this shit happened."

"A broken egg isn't gonna fix this, Dad, and a gypsy isn't the reason we get sick."

"Look at all the bad stuff that happen. How you think it happen?"

"Dad, that's not how it works."

The car pulled up to his house. He fumbled out of the car. Inside, he put on a small saucepan for the pasta. He ate dinner quietly in front of the TV. Cleaned his dishes. Turned off the TV.

///

"Thank you for coming in. We have the forms for you to sign and then we can meet with you individually to figure out payments for your interlock ignition. You can pick up your new license at any ICBC location." The teacher walked around to each student and handed out the forms.

"I don't know what any of this means. I wait for my son," he yelled to no one in particular.

His son walked into the class as everyone was packing up their belongings. The son started to talk with the teacher then waved his father over. He grunted, then walked to the front of the class.

"Dad, she's saying that you might not have to bother with the whole interlock ignition because of an amendment to the law."

"So I get my license?"

"It sounds like it."

"Okay."

He pulled at his thumb.

"I no want to pay for it anyway. Crooks take all my money."

The teacher and his son laughed. The son signed the papers on his behalf and ushered him to his car. "We'll stop by the insurance place on the way home."

"For what?"

"For your license."

"Nah, I don' need that today. We get it another time."

"Dad, you can start driving again."

"Nah, I don' need it. Don' worry about it. Okay, just take me home." He grabbed a book at his feet, "Another day," and threw it into the back seat. "I don' need it. Just take me home." He pulled at his thumb. His son turned up the radio. "I remember when I was your age, I listen to music and go out to the disco."

His son responded with silence.

"Back then, I even went to that disco where you go roller skating. I remember I was nineteen, and I just get here. I can no speak English, and Friday they give us a paycheque and we go out. We stay out all night, and then Sunday we drive around church to see if there was any girls who wanted to get married. You gotta go to church, that's where you find a girlfriend. You never have a girlfriend, you're getting too old, and no girls. You can't be alone. I'm alone now, and I know marriage was no good, but at least someone is there. Sure, you drive each other crazy, and we fight, but I dunno. I remember that, going out Sunday, driving around looking for girls, and then I meet your mother. Now I'm here. I dunno. I get my license and where do I go?"

"We can still pick it up."

"No. I have nowhere to go."

The car pulled up to his house. He waited for the car to pull away, then walked around to the back of the house. He lifted a small package from a planter, a mix of salt and pepper. He opened it, let it scatter across the backyard as rain trickled down. He put the key back into the packet and into the planter. Once inside, he put on a small saucepan for the pasta. He ate dinner quietly in front of the TV. Cleaned his dishes. Turned off the TV.

HANDSOME MEN

Mother

You know, I had a boyfriend that I met at the hospital once, it was just like this hospital. I was very sick, and this other man was in the bed across from me.

Me

I thought you only had that boyfriend before you met Dad.

Mother

No, I had another boyfriend. We only dated for a short time. He was so handsome. Really attractive. I was only sixteen, you know?

Me

How did he ask you out?

Mother

He just kept flirting with me while in the hospital. We were both in hospital gowns. Then finally he asked me out. Handsome men don't really need to hesitate to ask anyone out.

Me

I guess not. Why didn't it work out?

Mother

You can never trust handsome men.

Me

I know.

FAKE BOYFRIEND

Welcome to Fakeboyfriend.net. Would you like a boyfriend who texts you all the time, and ONLY has time for you? Sign up NOW for your first twenty texts free. Fakeboyfriend.net is here for you.

NEIL

Neil: So how does this work?

Anthony: Well, I can meet you for sushi, or we can go see a movie.

Neil: But you don't actually come to see the movie or eat with me?

Anthony: Um, well, I mean, I have all the time in the world for you.

Neil: So we just text?

Anthony: I am a really good listener.

Neil: What do you look like?

Anthony: I have brown hair, blue eyes, and I'm a surfer, so pretty fit.

Neil: I'm mostly into Asians.

Anthony: I forgot, I'm half Asian.

ERIK

Anthony pulled up to the café. He could see a guy texting on his phone who looked like the guy described. He sat in his car for a while, still texting him. "I'm here, where are you?" Erik texted back, "sitting at a table, join me."

Anthony unbuckled the seatbelt, wiped the sweat from his forehead, and got out of the car. He ordered a coffee and waited, without turning around to find

Erik. He wasn't ready to say "hello" until he was mentally prepared. The barista called out his order. He took the coffee and slowly walked toward the guy he was certain was Erik.

"Hi."

"Hello." Erik looked up from his phone.

"Um. I'm Anth—"

"Anthony, from fakeboyfriend.net."

"Yeah."

Anthony sat down and took a sip of his coffee, while Erik continued to look at his phone for a moment, then put his phone down; he was sweating. "So, this isn't, like, part of the service, is it? Like, you shouldn't be here?"

"Technically, no. And it would be great if you didn't report me. If they find out that I've visited one of my clients, they'll fire me right away."

Erik nodded and looked at his phone. The sweat from his palms made the cover slippery.

Anthony sighed and then finally perked up. "Did you know that one of the most common documented causes of breakups is not giving your relationship the proper title? We're so used to labelling everything, that when it's mislabelled, it can lead to broken hearts. Imagine someone mislabelled something at the grocery store, and you bought it, say hummus, but you wanted spinach dip. You'd return it, right?"

"Heh, yeah, I guess." Erik sipped his iced coffee.

"So, I guess we already kind of know each other a lot."

Erik smiled. "I guess you're right. How long do you think you'll have to work at fakeboyfriend.net until you finish your masters in Biology?"

"Oh, like a couple years at the most. I've had a lot of interest from employers."

"Sorry to sound stupid, but what does someone with a Masters in Biology do?"

"They mostly do research jobs."

Erik smiled. Anthony put down his mug and took some of the foam from the sides with his finger and licked it. He hadn't grabbed a napkin so he wiped his finger on his shorts.

The short coffee date turned into dinner that turned into drinks. Anthony refused the drinks but had a soda. Erik drank more and more until his hands were touching Anthony's lap.

"You want to come over?" Erik was slurring by now.

Anthony nodded.

KEVIN

Anthony: It's just for a coffee, I promise. Nothing weird.

Kevin: I just can't. Please. I don't feel well. I don't want to meet you.

Anthony: I promise I am just as nice in real life.

Kevin: I don't do well in public places. I just need to talk, please.

DAVE

Dave: Tell me you're sorry again.

Anthony: I'm sorry.

Dave: Like u mean it

Anthony: I'm so so sorry, i never meant to heart u
*hurt
*autocorrect

Dave: Thank you.

Anthony: I know this might be weird, but would you maybe want to

Dave: I didn't think that's how this
service worked.

meet in person?

Anthony: Well, it doesn't. But I
just think maybe we have a real
connection.

Dave: I don't know. That doesn't
feel right.
(...)

Dave: Okay. Or, just not right now.

Anthony: No worries. Just a thought.

ERIK

Erik: What are you up to?

Anthony: Just thinking about you.

Erik: :) You want to hang out this
week?

Anthony: Of course! You name the
place and time.

Erik: Sushi, Main Street?

Anthony: Perfect.

Erik: Wait, but we will actually hang
out, right? Like, you're not playing
fakeboyfriend right now and we will
actually meet?

JULIAN

Anthony waited outside Julian's place. He memorized the walkway, every
step that led to the doorway, the pathway that swooped around the entrance,
the plants that lined the windows. Julian came out of the basement suite door

on the west side of the house. He was tall, handsome, and very young. Much younger than Anthony'd expected.

Julian smiled at Anthony and walked over to the car. When he sat down, Anthony quickly mumbled, "How old are you?"

"I'm twenty-eight, like I told you."

"You're not twenty-eight."

"Okay, no. I'm twenty-five."

Anthony felt a twitch in his stomach that let him know Julian was still lying, but if he made too much of a fuss he might get caught breaking his contract. Anthony started to drive and asked Julian more questions.

"So, you like music?"

"I *love* music." Julian perked up.

"What musicians do you like? Like, No Doubt or maybe, say, One Direction?"

"Do I look like I'd be into One Direction?"

Anthony grabbed them seats near the back of the theatre. He was already paranoid enough about being caught on dates, but it was obvious that there was more than ten years between his current date and himself.

Julian put his hand on Anthony's lap. Anthony couldn't help but become aroused.

"Who's your favourite actor? Do you like, um, say, Chris Pine or are you more of a fan of Tom Cruise?"

"Is Tom Cruise the one who was in those *Speed* movies?"

Anthony nodded, not wanting to correct him. The movie started, and Julian's hand slipped up Anthony's thigh. He felt the button on his pants flick open and the pressure on his stomach released. Julian's cold hand slid down into his underwear and pulled on his dick. Anthony inhaled deeply and let Julian's head come down on his lap. "I'm not supposed to do this," Anthony whispered. There were only a few theatre goers, but they looked like they were in their late sixties and sat as close to the front as possible.

"You're not twenty-five, are you?"

Julian continued to tongue Anthony's head and slowly turned to say, "I might be twenty-two."

NEIL

Neil walked up toward the coffee shop. Anthony was sitting in a booth, texting on his phone.

"Another boyfriend?"

"Uh, yeah," Anthony giggled nervously.

"I am still weirded out by this, but I was intrigued."

"Intrigued how?"

Neil gave him an irritated look. "Oh, I don't know. Maybe someone using a weird fakeboyfriend site to find dates is just a bit ... weird."

"I don't use it to find dates."

"Right, so what is this?"

"I just wanted to meet for coffee. I like to see the fakeboyfriend's faces. It helps me provide a better service."

"Do you actually believe that?"

Anthony became hot with irritation. His skin warmed and sweat gathered on his forehead. "I do!"

"Right. Have you even had a real boyfriend before?"

"Yes! I've had several! I was even almost married once."

Neil laughed, "Well, then what happened—you found out he wasn't real?"

"Fuck you. We were happy. We were just—"

"What, not enough time to come up with your lie when there's no phone between us?"

"We lived in different cities and he, he couldn't move here."

"Sure."

"I don't have to prove anything to you."

"Okay, well, this has been enlightening, but I am done here." Neil got up to walk away, but turned back. "You're not even half Asian, are you?"

"It's what you wanted me to be."

Neil looked at the floor. Anthony could sense his sadness. "It's okay to pretend."

Neil walked out of the coffee shop.

ERIK

Erik: You never came to sushi yesterday.

> Anthony: Sure, I did. We had a great time.

JULIAN

Julian: Hi, this isn't Julian, this is his mother. It says on his phone that you are his boyfriend. Julian never told us he was gay. I do not know how else to say this but Julian passed away last night. I know we have never met but the family would like to meet you. This is a very tough time for me and our family and I would just like to know more about you. I'm sorry to be the one to tell you. — Maria

> Anthony: Let me know where I should meet you.

The entire house was filled with grieving women. Everyone was dressed in black. They led me into the kitchen where several older women were simultaneously cooking and cleaning. They sat him next to a woman with her head down in her arms. An older woman rubbed the back of her neck.

"Maria, he's here."

She looked up, and Anthony saw that her eyes were red and moist. She pulled Anthony's arm and grasped him into a desperate hug and wept. She wailed into his shoulder; Anthony had to hold on to her to keep her standing. He held her up as much as he could, and her weight pulled him down, but not his physical body; it felt as if his stomach was sinking and then he felt a weird rush that couldn't be held back. Anthony began to sob. He cried hard into her shoulder, holding her closer. Maria heaved great sobs, and they held each other for what felt like a half an hour but was probably not much more than a minute.

"I'm so sorry," Anthony apologized.

"I'm the one who's sorry. I never got to meet you. I never knew. He just never told me anything, and I don't know why."

A woman placed a big plate of food in front of Anthony. He looked up in confusion. The woman yelled, "You gotta eat something, you look starved."

"What is this?"

"Lasagna, you've never seen a lasagna before?"

"What is that, like a casserole?"

Maria grabbed his hands and started to laughing. "You're sweet. I see why Julian liked you."

ERIK

Anthony: Haven't heard from you in a while, should we go on another date?

Erik: ?

Anthony: It's your boyfriend, Anthony.

Erik: Oh, please. This has been
so messed up. I would like to
discontinue service.

> 87558: To discontinue service
> from fakeboyfriend.net please type
> DISCONTINUE SERVICE

Erik: DISCONTINUE SERVICE

> 87558: Thank you, we hope you
> have enjoyed fakeboyfriend.net. If
> you would ever like to return just
> type RETURN SERVICE

JULIAN

The limo pulled up to his apartment. It was followed by three more limos and a line of cars behind it. When he climbed inside, he saw that Maria's lap was filled with tissues. It was hard to see her with her body covered in long black clothing. No one spoke. The limo drove through several neighbourhoods before stopping at a small church. There were people lined up to get inside, and the crowd spilled out on to the street.

"Is this all for Julian?" Anthony asked.

"Julian was very much loved."

They walked slowly to the church. Anthony tried to slip into a pew near the back, but Maria grabbed his hand and ushered him to the front. The service was delivered half in Italian so Anthony dropped his head and just listened to the way the entire church joined in the prayers and how the language echoed back and forth. A wave of consonants and hissing s's rolled around Anthony's head. When the service was over, the people lined up to visit the open casket and kiss the cheeks of everyone in the first row. He felt every soft kiss as they whispered their condolences to him. The family took turns breaking down with each kiss.

The line finally dwindled down and the churchgoers filled the streets.

He and Maria returned to the limo, and it drove through the suburbs toward a large cemetery. It pulled up to an old mausoleum which looked as if it had been licked by flames. The crowd moved inside and stood against the walls. Anthony looked up to see crypts stacked from the floor to ceiling. Julian's casket was moved into the centre of the space. With barely any room to move, the priest spoke to the mourners, praying and asking each person to come and place ashes upon Julian's casket.

Anthony joined the line with Maria and grabbed a pinch of ashes, then sprinkled them on the casket. He started to cry; he felt the weight of his body become too much for his legs. Anthony hugged Maria and said, "I didn't know Julian that well. I don't belong here."

"You belong here, you belong here," she repeated over and over again. "I didn't know Julian that well either," said his mother.

When they left the mausoleum, Anthony noticed a few lit candles in a long row of candles. He stopped and stared.

"You light a candle as a prayer. In my family, we light one for each person we lost." Maria picked up a long thin stick and lit the end on fire. "Here."

Anthony lit a candle and thanked Maria.

"No, thank you. I would have loved to see Julian so happy with you."

As he was leaving, Anthony heard Maria rush up quickly behind him. "You have to come to dinner next Sunday! We have a big family dinner every Sunday."

Anthony clutched his jacket and stammered, "I, I'd love that."

ERIK

Anthony: Glad we had such a great
sushi date last night.

Erik: What the fuck are you doing?
I cancelled your services. You can't
charge me for this shit.

Anthony: It was, uh, a joke. Thought
I would try again. Maybe we can
have Italian? It would be as friends.
I kind of need someone to talk to.

Erik: ...

Erik: Fine. But JUST a coffee.

Anthony: That's perfect. I promise
it won't be anything more than a
friendly chat. I'm kind of dating
someone. He's nice. His name is
Julian.

i talked to you again on the phone. you were in the hospital and could only have one more visitor. i was confused. my sisters had made it clear that you were dead, but i could hear your voice on the phone. someone said i could visit tomorrow because it was getting bad, but i would get just one more visit. i was begging you to hold on for one more day so i could see you again. the day slowed down infinitely so that the next day never came. you waited in the hospital bed, and i waited for tomorrow.

NICE SHORTS, BRO

Kevin looked down, focusing on his steps, making sure he was walking a straight line, each step, neatly in front of the other. His hair was slightly matted and parted to the side, his shirt perfectly ironed, tucked into his shorts with a skinny belt that matched his shoes. His shorts, a light Easter blue, were rolled up twice because they were a bit too long for his short legs. Kevin checked the crease on his shorts to make sure they weren't bunching up awkwardly, as they tended to. He looked up to see an older woman walking in his direct path on the left side of the sidewalk. He quickly shuffled to the other side, apologized to her, then shuffled back.

He walked into the coffee shop, ordered his sandwich, and quietly waited for his soy latte. He stared down at the floor between the condiments table and the counter where they would usually place his coffee. As people came to get sugar for their coffee, he awkwardly slipped to the side, saying, "sorry."

"Latte and sandwich to go!"

"That's for me, thanks." He took a sip, noticed it was milk, and continued to smile. He grabbed his sandwich and walked out the door.

His face began to sweat as he sipped the latte. He noticed someone coming toward him but didn't recognize the man's face, so went back to staring at the ground. Kevin didn't want to be rude to someone he might know, but he also didn't want to make eye contact with someone he didn't know. He wasn't certain if he knew him, so he looked up again: no, it wasn't someone he knew. He looked down again in case they made eye contact.

"Nice shorts, bro," he heard the man say.

He looked up again to see if he knew the guy, but it was a stranger. A young jock, smiling. "Thank you," was all he could mumble out. He began to replay the interaction over and over again, each time losing his certainty that he was wearing nice shorts. He certainly wasn't a bro. He looked at his shorts. Plain blue shorts, rolled twice. Not too short to be offensive. Definitely not the shorts of a bro. Maybe the shorts were a little too tight. He had gained weight since he bought them, maybe a few pounds, but he also knew he wasn't that noticeably bigger than usual. Maybe they were too fancy. He did feel uncomfortable that he'd purchased them from a popular store. He could feel sweat dripping down his lower back. He felt pretty fucking stupid in these shorts right now.

When he arrived back at the office, he was covered in sweat. His co-worker stopped him to ask a question, but Kevin mumbled something and ran to the bathroom.

"You got another milk latte didn't you?" his co-worker yelled after him.

An uncomfortably long moment later, he went back to his desk. He typed out the words, "nice shorts bro." He placed a comma between the nice shorts and bro, then added an exclamation mark. "nice shorts, bro!" Or maybe it was, "nice, shorts bro."

Stevie looked over. "Kevin can you send me the databa—"

"If someone said 'nice shorts, bro,' would you think they were making fun of your shorts or liked your shorts?"

"Uh, I'm not sure. Your shorts seem fine. I doubt they were making fun of you."

"But ... he was 'straight,' you know."

"Kevin, no one's making fun of your shorts."

"But he was like a jock guy."

"Kevin, can you just send me that database?"

After a series of database inputs in several Excel documents, Kevin looked up to see that it was 4:45, so there were only fifteen minutes left of work. He began to close down his applications. He needed to be at dinner with his mother by eight. This left him three hours to get to the gym, shower, and take a bus so he'd be early for dinner. He repeated the plan: gym, shower, bus, dinner. He began thinking about the gym. The lineups to get to the cardio machines. The extensive amount of men in the weight room. The gym didn't normally die down until seven. He thought: shower, light gym, bus, dinner.

No, he couldn't shower before the gym; he would go to the gym, but just use the broken treadmill no one ever used and skip the weights. He thought of the clicking noise the treadmill made when he ran. He thought about his upper body muscles withering away from not doing any weights. He thought about going to the gym and everyone noticing that he was only there for ten minutes and how they would think, "That's weird. Why did he work out for only ten minutes?" He looked up at the clock. It was now 5:05. He had to make a decision. He could bring his clothes to the gym and shower there. He thought of the shower floors, how busy the shower always are, and being naked in front of strangers. He thought about how he would have to bring a big bottle of soap to the shower. Everyone would look at him and think, "Why does he have such a large bottle of soap?" He looked up again, 5:15. *Who would make fun of someone's shorts? It had to be a compliment.* Gym, no shower, bus, then dinner. 5:20. Today was a gym day; if he didn't go today it would mean that he would have to go tomorrow, and then his whole schedule would shift. Bus, dinner, gym, shower. He clicked between his personal email and his work emails, not really reading either of them. The click of the treadmill. Click. The soap bottle. Click. 5:30. The office lights turned off. He looked up to see his co-worker waiting at the door to let him out. He quickly packed up.

"Sorry," Kevin said.

"You know, you really need to tell those baristas you're lactose intolerant."

The gym was busy. Busier than usual. He quickly shuffled to the locker room and changed in the corner. He tripped over his shorts trying to get them on as quickly as possible. He wandered over to the treadmill section. Busy. There was the broken treadmill. It worked perfectly fine, except for that clicking. He thought about just changing and leaving again. He shook his head and walked over to the treadmill. He started it slow, so that it only clicked about every second or so. The click wasn't too noticeable today. He thought maybe they'd fixed it. He relaxed and turned the speed up. The clicking increased slightly. It was clicking more than once per second. He tried to drown it out by playing music. Click. He fumbled with his earphones. Click. Someone looked toward him. Click. He pressed stop. He looked around; it felt as though the treadmill was still clicking. He ran toward the locker room, grabbed his things, and texted his mother. "I can't make it today, I'm not feeling well."

///

He was aware of the handcuffs he'd placed on himself and the handkerchief with which he'd covered his eyes. His bedroom door opened, and he felt him slide into him quickly. A searing pain rose from his spine.

"Thank you," he whispered.

///

Kevin's office opened at nine, but he always waited patiently at 8:45 for the first person with a key to come and open the doors. He had been adamant that he did not want a key to the office, worried that would lead to more responsibility.

When Stevie arrived and let him in, Kevin rushed into the bathroom, locked the doors, and began to unpeel a section of wallpaper under a poster showing a group of business people smiling and raising their hands. He found his spot and doodled with a black felt pen for thirteen minutes—enough time to make the office think he was having his morning movement, but not long enough to question if he was wasting time jerking off. When his phone vibrated, he put the wallpaper back, taped the poster back up, flushed the toilet, and sprayed the bathroom with berry-scented air freshener.

Back at his desk, he asked Stevie, "Do you think he was making fun of me?"

"Oh god, for saying you have nice shorts?"

"Who just compliments someone's shorts?"

"Someone who likes shorts."

He looked at Stevie for a long time without saying anything.

"You have to stop staring at me now," said Stevie.

Kevin opened a new Excel document, and as he did so he noticed a weird yellowish bruise on his finger. It was small, but he felt a slight pain when he pressed hard against it. He Googled, "yellow bruise on finger," found eight diseases for finger bruises, and clicked through to "blood infection" and then to "gonorrhea." He called his doctor to schedule an appointment.

Next, Kevin began to compose an email to himself, a tactic his therapist had asked him to use whenever he was feeling anxious or angry. It was now a daily routine. He would write whatever he was feeling in an email, send it to himself, then read it again.

Dear Kevin,

Nice shorts bro! Nice, shorts bro. Nice shorts, bro. Nice shorts bro?! Nice, shorts, bro. Nice. Shorts bro! NICE SHORTS BRO. Nice. Shorts. Bro. Nice shorts bro. Nice shorts bro. Nice shorts, bro? Nice? Shorts. Bro?

Nice shorts bro,

Kevin.

ps. Nice shorts bro.

pps. Nice shorts, bro.

ppps. Fuck you Stevie.

He hit send.

He clicked the "get mail" button, waiting for his email to pop up. He figured there must be a server problem holding the email back. He clicked "get mail" again. He began to click it several times, with increased intensity. His face was soon covered with a cold film of sweat. "Get mail." Click, click, click, "get mail." He went into the sent email folder and found the problem. He had emailed Stevie instead of himself. He looked over to her computer, but she was in the bathroom. He shifted over to her seat. The computer was locked. He could hear her coming back. He pushed the computer off her desk onto the ground. It landed with a gentle thud on the carpet.

"Fuck." A long moan slipped from his mouth.

He put the computer back, rushed over to his computer, and typed furiously.

Dear Stevie,

Did you like my joke? So funny. Nice shorts bro? Hahahaha. LOLOLOLOLOLOL

Kevin

And another email.

HA-HA STEVIE, SO FUNNY! LOL Fuck you. HAHAHA
Kevin

And another.

What are you doing for lunch? We should go get coffee. Ha ha, fuck you. HAHAHA.
Kevin

He turned off his computer screen and quietly slipped outside.

///

Kevin looked up to see the young man who had complimented his shorts. He ducked behind a tree as the man passed him. He slowly came from behind the tree and followed him. He was wearing a Whole Foods employee polo and heading toward the store. Kevin slinked behind him, making sure he wasn't noticed.

Kevin quickly lined up at the coffee station, so as not to appear like he was following the man. Nice Shorts Bro had gone through a door, probably to the back of the building.

"Soy latte, please."

He ordered without looking at the server, still focusing on the door that Nice Shorts Bro had gone into. He wasn't coming back out.

"Latte for Kevin."

He grabbed the coffee and rushed back to work. As he sipped the searing hot coffee, he could taste the dairy.

///

The gym. Click. The milk. Click. His face was paralyzed. Nice shorts, bro. Click. The door opened and closed. The lock, click.

"Tell me what to do."

He felt strong hands under his waist, gripping his ass, and pulling him forward.

"Tell me what to do," he repeated.

"Hold your ankles while I tie them."

His mind cleared. He could see clouds. Soy milk being frothed like the sky. His chest opened up. His body became warm.

///

"Can we talk about the emails you sent Stevie?"

Kevin was sitting in a small office with his boss and two computers showing two people he had never met before on the screens.

"I meant them as a joke."

"And we understand that, but as a rule, we have to meet with you about it."

Kevin's shirt was covered in sweat. He nodded.

One of the people on the computers said, "Kevin, we need to ask you a few standard questions. First, do you have any thoughts of hurting your fellow employees?"

Kevin shook his head.

"Sorry, Kevin, we are going to need you to state your answers for HR purposes."

"No."

"Have you ever had any negative thoughts toward one of your fellow employees?"

"No."

Kevin could feel the dairy from the latte hit him. His stomach and his bowels felt like they were stretching apart. He turned pale.

"Kevin, are you okay?"

Kevin nodded.

"Okay, have you ever thought of physically assaulting any of your fellow employees?"

"No."

"Have you ever physically hurt another human being?"

"No."

"Have you ever physically hurt an animal?"

"No, well, no. But ...?" Kevin was now visibly sweaty.

"Sorry, Kevin, can you answer with a yes or no."

"I, uh. Yes, but no. I was a kid. I didn't want to. My friend made me, we had a pellet gun. It was a small rabbit. I don't know if I ... I don't know if I hit it."

"That's okay, Kevin. We can move on to our next set of questions."

The pain in Kevin's stomach was beginning to deafen him.

"Did you ever make any unwanted sexual advances toward a fellow employee?"

Kevin leaned forward holding his stomach. He rushed out of the room without responding.

///

Kevin lay on the bathroom floor for over an hour. After the pain subsided, he sat on the toilet and imagined he was in a cabin, deep in the forest. The cabin was small, but it was filled with soymilk and a treadmill that didn't click when he ran on it, and there was that guy, telling him how nice his shorts were. Kevin asked him, "Do you really like my shorts?"

Brodude: "Yeah, man, those shorts are super rad."

Kevin: "Even the way I folded them up twice?"

Brodude: "They make you look incredibly sexy and relaxed."

Kevin: "What about me?"

Brodude: "You are so relaxed and chill. I am totally straight, but when I'm around you, I'm very, very gay."

There was a heavy knock on the door.

"Kevin, are you okay? Everyone is worried that you passed out."

It was Stevie. Kevin slowly crept up off the floor to open the door.

"What do you want?" Kevin asked.

"Just wanted to make sure you were okay."

"Right, except for reporting me to the managers."

"I never told them about the emails. Any email with swearwords is automatically sent to head office."

He didn't trust Stevie. He knew what a bitch she could be. Stevie was out to get him. He knew it. He remembered all the times she didn't respond to his questions.

///

The managers left Kevin alone for the next couple of days, but he knew they would be letting him go. He took more coffee breaks than normal, lurking around the coffee shop to see if Brodude would be there. He was working through the plan. He would go up to him and curtly say, "Nice shorts, bro." He would be really cold about it. Just "Nice shorts bro" and then walk away, as if it meant nothing. It was sooner than he expected when Brodude walked up to him at the coffee shop and said hello. All Kevin could do was mumble, "Nice shorts bro."

"Sorry, what?"

"Nothing." Kevin went quiet.

"No, you said something. I just couldn't hear you."

"I just, I was saying, I was wearing shorts one day."

"Sorry, what?"

"Sometimes I wear shorts, and they're nice, I guess."

"Oh, yeah, you had those nice shorts."

"You remember?"

"Yeah, they were yellow or something?"

"Blue."

"Right, blue! Plus your legs looked really good in them."

"Oh." Kevin looked at the ground.

"This is probably weird, and I'm not even sure if you're gay, but if you are, would you want to go grab a drink some time?"

Kevin stared blankly for what felt like several minutes. He slowly let a "yes" slip out of his mouth.

"Cool. Well, I'm off work later, so catch me then and we can go from there."

Kevin nodded without being able to get a word out. His latte was put on the counter. Kevin grabbed the latte, took a sip, and tasted the dairy. He felt something bubble up inside him that he'd never felt before.

Click.

"I am *lactose intolerant*. I am fucking *lactose intolerant!* This makes me instantly *shit!*" He threw the coffee against the window. The moment the cup left his hands, his rage dissipated. He looked over to Brodude, then ran back toward the office. He sat back in his chair and took deep breaths. There was a post-it note on his screen with "goodbye" and a sad face written on it. He ripped it off in a rage, then began to type.

To whom it may concern:
It pains me to report that I will no longer be working here. I don't feel safe here. I don't feel respected. I work VERY hard, and I can tell you all want me to go.
Kevin

Kevin turned off his computer. He ran past the desks, noticing brightly coloured post-it notes on all of the computer screens. He imagined that all of the notes said something terrible about him. Each one would reveal his secrets. Each flashed in his head. Click. The moments collapsed on him. Click. He thought of the dead rabbit. Click. He followed the post-it notes into the copy room. Hundreds of pages had come out of the copier. "I feel weird" was typed on each page. He collapsed to the ground.

"Kevin, are you okay?" He could hear Stevie behind him.

"I feel weird," he replied.

///

The door opened; he could hear the lock click afterward. The familiar sound of thick, hard boots dampened by carpet as they came up the steps. His bedroom door opened. He felt nails scratch hard down his back.

"What do you want me to do with these little blue shorts?"

"I need you to rip them off me."

DATE: HARLEYQUEEN

Ryan walked him home; it was pouring rain and both of them had forgotten an umbrella. HarleyQueen invited him in, and they sat on two small sofas. HarleyQueen poured them water, and Ryan gulped it down, hoping it would sober him up. Ryan looked around and noticed all of the comic-book character figurines.

"You like comic books?"

HarleyQueen laughed. "Yeah, obviously."

Ryan got up to look at one of the display cases; it had figurines of a female character wearing a jester outfit and a wide smile. "Who is this?"

"Oh, that's Harley Quinn."

"I don't think I've ever heard of her before. Is she some sort of superhero?"

"Well, yes and no."

HarleyQueen motioned for Ryan to sit on the sofa with him. It was too small for both of them, so Ryan was forced to sit on his lap. The warmth of HarleyQueen's body made him feel at ease and a little sleepy.

"Harley is most famous for being Joker's girlfriend, but I really like the character. She was originally an intern at the insane asylum that Joker was in, and she became his psychiatrist. She quickly falls in love with him because he's actually really charming. He's really manipulative, too, so she becomes infatuated with him and helps him escape. Then it becomes clear that he's just using her, and so she goes insane."

Ryan's head was now lying in HarleyQueen's lap. He was having trouble breathing, and tears were quickly welling up. He asked HarleyQueen for another glass of water. While he was in the kitchen, Ryan wiped away the tears and calmed down with his breathing techniques. HarleyQueen was smiling when he came back; he leaned over and kissed Ryan. The two were pressed against the small couch. As Ryan began to pull his clothes off and they continued to kiss, HarleyQueen pushed back hard and aggressively. Ryan felt the room shake. They moved off the couch and slammed against a wall. He could see and hear picture frames dropping to the floor. Ryan felt someone else grip his neck, but the room was empty except for the two of them. His rage made him focus harder on HarleyQueen. He pushed his hands down his pants and in that moment, he experienced a wave a pleasure rise in him. The furniture was floating, the doors and cabinet doors were slamming open and closed, and comic books were flying off the shelves.

"Stop!" HarleyQueen pushed Ryan back. He looked around the room, now covered in comic books and strewn clothing. "I should be good. You need to go."

Ryan stared at him awkwardly but nodded.

"Quickly. You have to leave right away. I'm sorry."

Ryan looked outside and noticed the downpour. He looked back as the door closed on him and walked into the rain.

THE BREAK

We see a blurry shot of a man with his head down; he is crying. The image flips and there is a flash of Jacob crying as well. The scene changes—it's Jacob walking down Church Street with papers in his hand, while soft indie rock plays as the soundtrack. Jacob enters a small bar, and a few friends wave at him. He turns to the camera, laughs, and pushes it away from him. The screen fades to white and opens over a Los Angeles street with palm trees and muscle men working out on a beach. The screen fades to white and the words, "The Break" appear. The screen again fades to white.

Jacob enters a small apartment with white furniture, overlooking a beach. Palm trees are seen in the distance from the window.

"So, they brought me to L.A. to do some auditions. This is the first time I've been to L.A. for work. My agent has been booking me auditions steadily since my video went viral on YouTube. We're here for pilot week, and today is a big day for that. I am in auditions all week long, so I better get ready because I really have a good feeling about this."

The camera spins rapidly away and spins back to Jacob sitting in the back of a car, going over his lines. He mumbles to himself, then looks at the camera, smiles nervously, then continues to whisper lines to himself. The camera spins again to show him sitting in an audition waiting room where there are several handsome men in tight shirts that reveal their muscles. Jacob is considerably smaller than the other men.

"Guess I better get back to the gym," Jacob laughs. He continues to look over his lines and shakes his hands out, nervously. He shakes them out over and over again and begins to pace back and forth.

Fade to white.

Jacob is sitting in a cab, wiping sweat from his forehead. "So, I think I did really well at that audition. I've always been very good at auditions, but I can guess that I won't get the part. They were looking for someone much bigger than me, but that's okay. I'm not meant to get those parts. I'll need time to bulk up like that, and I'm not even sure if I want to. Like, maybe I am just not that kind of guy, maybe that's not my brand."

Palm trees speed by as the sun flickers through them.

Jacob is now walking into an office with his agent. She has long black hair; it reaches all the way down her back and is coloured with pastel-blue streaks. Her suit is grey, and the sound of her heels overwhelms the office as they step up to the receptionist. Then we hear Jacob's voiceover: "They had a special surprise for me. I actually have a role already settled today, so we are quickly going into the sound room for that. We'll be recording my voice for a commercial. I play a wrench who is helping to fix a car. It's very cute. It'll be my first commercial since that tragic marshmallow commercial I did a couple years ago."

Cut to a slightly younger Jacob slamming marshmallow after marshmallow into his mouth. Camera cuts back to Jacob with an irritated look on his face. "Please do *not* play that commercial for the show." Off-camera, we hear the agent and the producer laugh.

The camera follows Jacob and his agent into a recording room. A bearded older man sits behind the control board. He asks Jacob to try to make his best "wrench" voice. Jacob tries several voices, but the guy in the sound booth shakes his head at each one. After several attempts, Jacob uses his normal voice and improvises statements: "I'm a wrench, so let me grip your nuts!" The room erupts in laughter.

The camera quickly scans over palm trees. The sun sets at an accelerated pace, the moon rises quickly, and the street lights turn on. Jacob is putting on a collared shirt and gelling his hair. "I figure, since I haven't gone out yet, it would be cool to see what the nightlife is here in L.A. I'd love to go out and have some drinks, and my agent has invited over some of her friends who I might get along with." There is the sound of knocking at the door. "Well, how's that for timing?" Jacob looks in the mirror, fixes a strand of hair, and walks into the living room. The agent opens the door. Some of the men who come in are those who tried out for the audition, and Jacob laughs in recognition. He greets each man, and they exchange names. The agent and her friends sit on a long white leather couch that stretches the length of the room. They're drinking a lot, and Jacob hands out shots. They all take a shot.

The camera focuses in close on Jacob and a blond man talking. "So, what do you do?" Jacob asks.

"I work in modelling. I've been trying to switch into acting, but it's not been an easy transition."

"Cool," Jacob smiles and touches the man's arm. Jacob stands up and speaks loudly to everyone in the room. "There's a limo outside waiting for us—should we head out on the town?" The men all cheer and take a shot before they pour out of the apartment and pack into the limo.

The camera spins over a night club scene; it's too loud for conversation, and the men have all split up. Jacob is sitting alone on a plush couch. A server comes by. The words "Do you want another drink?" appear onscreen. The sound of music makes it impossible to hear his response. The server walks away.

A few women dance in front of him. The server returns with his drink, and Jacob downs it fast. The server comes back and he nods. Another drink is placed on the table next to him.

The scene changes to Jacob dancing with strangers, slowly grinding against someone who looks uncomfortable, then walks away. He goes to the bar, orders a shot. He takes the shot with the bartender.

The scene changes to later in the night. Jacob is dancing on stage next to a go-go boy dancer who's trying to push him off the stage.

The camera follows Jacob as he suddenly leaves the bar. He yells at the producer to turn the camera off, then runs behind a large garbage container. The producer walks into the shot. The conversation is muffled. The words "I don't want to do this anymore" appear on the screen.

Producer: "Let's just get you home."

Jacob: "I want to go home."

Producer: "You just drank too much."

Jacob: "No, I f***ing want to go home."

The scene fades to white.

The scene opens on Jacob's apartment. His clothes are scattered around the room. Wearing only his underwear, Jacob lies on his bed. His voice is heard: "So, I probably had too much to drink last night, and I talked to the producers. We worked everything out. I can sometimes be a total drama queen. But I just need to get myself together today because I have a few more auditions for pilot season. But more exciting than that, my agent has also decided to set me up on a couple of dates! I haven't really been dating lately because I have been *so* focused on my career, but I figure this would be a nice way to break up my day full of auditions. My first date is with Kieran, the nice blond guy I met last night, and I couldn't be more excited."

The scene spins to a coffee shop. Kieran is sitting with a coffee. Jacob walks up and gives Kieran a hug. The scene awkwardly cuts to mid-conversation.

"What happened last night?" Kieran asks.

"Oh, I drank a little too much. Where did you head off to?"

"I had an early audition, so I had to leave early."

The camera focuses in on Jacob's hands; he's clutching his fingers tightly in one of his palms.

"So, Kieran, what brought you to Hollywood?"

"I was working in New York. I'd been modelling for some time. My family grew up in Brooklyn, so I wasn't far away from home at all. Well, about a couple years ago I came out to my family. My mom took it really bad and my father stopped talking to me." Light but somber music begins to play. "My mom was always my number-one fan, and she told me I could do anything I wanted. I realized that I wanted to get into acting and not just model, so I booked a flight, sold all of my belongings, and came here. My mom still keeps in touch, and we're doing better now. My dad still hasn't really talked to me since."

Jacob reaches for Kieran's hand and the camera zooms in on their clasped hands. Kieran wipes away tears from his left eye, then perks up. "So, what brought you to L.A.?"

Jacob smiles. "I've been acting in Canada for so long and really hit a glass ceiling, so my agent thought it would be great to send me to L.A. You know, after my YouTube video went viral."

"That's right!" Kieran laughs excitedly. "I remember watching that video all the time. It was totally crazy. Rumours are going around that it's fake."

"I mean, it was a little set-up, I guess. But mostly real."

"That's f------ wild. I mean, I could never do that, but you really went for it, and it totally paid off."

Jacob and Kieran continue to talk and indie-rock music plays over the scene until the two get up and walk outside. They hug and wave goodbye.

"We should do this again," Kieran says.

The scene spins quickly to Jacob in a cab. "I'm really happy about that date. Kieran seems like a really nice and cool guy, and it was cool that he could talk about his mother with me. I really respect that." Jacob looks out the window.

The scene cuts to an office building. Jacob says in voiceover: "I'm stopping by a quick audition for a new show about teenagers who've just graduated high school. I'm pretty hopeful about this one because I think I can really pull off a teenager—I've always had a youthful look." The camera spins away and back to show Jacob walk out of the office building and give the camera a thumbs up.

The camera pans over Los Angeles and cuts back to Jacob's apartment. Jacob is dressing up. "There is apparently one more surprise for me tonight. I have had such a full day of work, and I had a great time with Kieran, so I'm a little exhausted, but I can't wait to see who I get to meet for dinner. It's a special blind date." Kieran looks at the mirror one last time and then walks toward the apartment door.

The camera cuts to a small restaurant. Jacob is rubbing his arms. He looks at the menu and looks at the front entrance. He does this several times until Dave is seen outside, walking up to the restaurant. Dave walks through the restaurant and sits at Jacob's table. Jacob appears uncomfortable; he continues to rub his hands and arms under the table. He looks at the camera, then just past the camera, and mouths the words "what the fuck?"

Dave sits quietly and asks the waitress for a whiskey.

"How have you been?" Dave asks Jacob.

Jacob stares off into the distance. He mumbles the word "Fine."

Dave smiles at Jacob. "It's okay. I'm not here to fight with you. I just wanted to see how you were doing."

"Fine," Jacob repeats.

"Well, you finally got what you wanted."

"If you're going to be an a–hole, then I'm not doing this."

"No, I'm sorry—I didn't mean it to come out like that. I'm honestly really happy that you're here. They tell me you're going on auditions, and I hear they're going well."

"It is." Jacob has tears welling up in his eyes. "I'm really sorry, I—"

"Stop, you're not that sorry. Look what it got you. And if you were really sorry, you would have taken that video down when I asked." Dave puts his hand on Jacob's hand and whispers, "You don't have to do this."

Jacob smirks then looks directly at Dave. "You would like that, wouldn't you, that I just go back to not existing?"

Dave gets even closer to Jacob. His words are hard to hear. We see words on the screen: "I know you. This isn't you. Why are you doing this?"

Jacob whispers back; it is inaudible, so the text appears on screen: "I did it because my agent hadn't called me in nine months, and I just felt like I was supposed to be someone. And ..." Jacob takes a long breath, "my agent said I had to do something big."

Dave looks away. He finishes the rest of his whiskey, then says, "Well, are you f--- happy?"

"Dave."

"What? Are you happy?"

"I'm the happiest I've been in so long."

Dave stares directly at Jacob then lowers his gaze down to his lap. He presses his fingers to his eyes, wipes his cheeks. "I forgive you," Dave says as he gets up.

Jacob stares at the menu until Dave walks away.

"F---." .

The scene cuts to Jacob outside of the restaurant having a smoke. He paces back and forth. He kicks a nearby postage box and says, "F---." The scene cuts to Jacob in a cab, looking at his phone, talking out loud. "The last thing he ever texted me was, 'who was this for?' and that was eight months ago. I never texted him back because I honestly didn't know the answer. I'm still not sure."

The camera cuts to Jacob getting ready for bed. He turns on his phone and plays a video. The sounds of Dave crying and begging him to stay repeat, over and over again. Jacob replays the entire video, then plays it one more time. His face is illuminated by the phone. The camera pulls away. Jacob's glowing face blurs and expands in the frame. The glow from his face grows to cover the screen. The screen fades to white.

Credits roll.

we took your flesh and built you back up again using a metal frame, you looked exactly the same, just smaller. sometimes, when i would hold you, i could hear your heart beat, but it was just the metal frame, clicking against itself.

SLIPS

He flips through her dresses, which are in a room built just for her clothes. He slides his hand over the fabrics. The room still smells of the oils from her skin. He finds the jewels she always wore, the shoes she never wore, the dresses she was saving for special occasions.

He gets back into the limo that drives them past her first home, her mother's home, the park they used to play in, the schools they went to, and finally to the cemetery she will be buried in.

When he arrives home, he unpacks his luggage. He pulls out the dresses, all the ones she never wore, with the jewels, the shoes, and places them on his bed. Organizes them they way she would have.

He puts them on one by one, pinching in the sides because they fit a little too wide and are a little too short. He chooses the red one and picks out the nail polish to match. He remembers the way she would polish her nails in the car when she drove them to school. The way she would drive slower than the speed limit, careful.

He cinches the dress tightly to his body using a stapler, then puts the final touches on his makeup. He picks up the square-cut aqua gem necklace and the matching ring and rubs them gently against his duvet to polish them. The necklace falls high on his collar bone with his hair rustling against it. The ring fits snugly on his pinky finger.

She takes a final look in the mirror and smiles, notices lipstick on her teeth, and wipes it off with a towel.

She makes her way to a dimly lit hotel bar, checks her phone, has a drink. She feels the dizziness of Prosecco on an empty stomach. She orders another, clinking the gem ring against the tall fluted glass. She orders a third drink, flirts with the waiter, pays her bill, and slides off the thick leather pub stool. The dark hotel bar feels like it will swallow her if she doesn't escape it soon.

She stumbles through the back door of The Odyssey. The club smells sour and sweet from the cran-and-vodka soaked carpets. A drag queen asks who she is, so she thinks of a lie and says she's new in town. She awkwardly holds out her hand to be kissed. The drag queen laughs and says, "We double kiss; we don't do hand gestures." She orders a whiskey, and the bartender doesn't charge her. She smiles and walks to the back to watch the men dance. Another drag queen walks up to her and asks her name. The drag queen asks if she has performed here before. She lies and says yes. The drag queen touches her hand and says that if she came by her house, she could help her with her nails. She looks down and notices that there is polish on the skin around some of her nails and absent from the tips of other nails.

She thinks about the way her mother used to paint her nails but clean them off before his father came home. Each night, her little-boy hands would be painted with all the shades of red the mother owned. The polish looked thick with glitter, folding in on itself in the bottle, swirled like lava.

She walks back home but doesn't go upstairs. She gets in her car and drives. She feels the pull toward her old home. She thinks about how if she had just driven there five days earlier, she could have asked her mother what it would be like to stay. She is driving five days back in time. She knows that she can do this, or she thinks she can, or she can at least drive fast enough to pause time so that it doesn't take her mother further away. The world in front of the windshield is blurry. She rolls down her window to smoke. Her car weaves and hits parked cars, knocking off mirrors and scraping paint off doors.

The summer heat keeps the night air from cooling her down. The sweat reminds her of the time she was feverish and her mother had to take care of all of the kids single-handedly, carrying their dizzy bodies to the bathroom, pressing damp towels to their heads.

She doesn't see the stop sign, and another car glides through it, hits her front wheel, and spins her into the house on the corner of the street.

Blood trickles down her hands. It's the same colour red she painted on her nails. A small glowing particle floats around his head. He tries to grab it, but it slips out the window. It took something from him, and he can't figure out what. Time hasn't stopped like he had hoped. When he rolls out of the car, the dress is missing. He doesn't ever really remember putting it on. The summer wind blows cold on his arms, sticky and wet. It lets the dark sail in.

DREAM BOY

the house is filled with old, empty boxes. i wander around trying to find you again, but it's just old empty boxes, and the boxes pile up and pile up. in the next room is a house party; it's a kitchen filled with strangers. a man grabs my phone. he is handsome and strong, but i let him take my phone. he takes a selfie. i wake up with my phone in my hand, and i'm sleeping on a plane that bucks and shakes. the pilot asks everyone to close their eyes as we nosedive into the ground

///

I felt a sharp corner poking into my stomach as I turned over in bed. My phone was lodged between my underwear and undershirt. I pulled it up to my face, unlocked it with one eye open. Scrolled through a group text.

CD: "Danny, wake the fuck up."

RB: "Butthead, we are going for brunch, get up"

I typed out with my thumb, "k, getting up rn."

C and R were waiting in line at the front of the restaurant. C pulled me under his armpit and put me in a tight hold.

"I haven't showered yet, smell the ripeness."

"You're fucking disgusting, C."

"No, lineups for brunch are fucking disgusting."

We settled into a booth, and I slid open the screen of my phone.

"Hey, I want you to check this out. Last night, I had this dream."

"Danny, no one cares about people's dreams. It's boring."

"I know, I know! But I had this dream where a hot guy took a photo of himself on my phone."

"So?" R was hungover and rubbing his eyes.

"So—look how hot he is!" I pulled my phone out to show them the most recent. The edges of the image were pitch-black, but a scruffy handsome man with bright green eyes was visible.

"Danny, he's just alright, and I keep telling you, talking about dreams is like trying to tell people about your childhood. It's only interesting to you."

I scrunched back into my seat and zoomed into his face. "I need a drink."

///

we walk through the amusement park. it's the dead of winter, and no one is on the rides, but they're still working. you take me to the wooden roller coaster. we ride for hours. the wooden tracks wobble and break open, and we fall into the earth

///

I woke up well past my alarm—it was 1:30 in the afternoon, and I was already late for a meeting. A cold panic hit me as I quickly showered and headed out the door.

When I pulled up to the coffee shop, the team was halfway through the meeting.

"Daniel, you're an hour and a half late."

"Sorry, I completely slept in."

"Were you out late last night?"

"No, it's just that, I met this guy and we've been really hitting it off."

"Where did you meet him?"

"In my dreams."

"Well, that's not much of an excuse for being so late. You literally sleep every night, and our meetings are only once a week."

I nodded. I opened my phone and flipped through the images. There was a short video of us on the wooden roller coaster. I slid the photo right, and there was a photo of us on the carousel. The head of the unicorn we were sitting on was lopped off. I giggled.

"Could you please pay attention? We are almost done budgeting for the year."

"Yeah, sorry."

///

we were in a house. it was completely empty. the house began to move upward; it was an elevator the size of an entire apartment. i could see the earth moving by the windows, dirt pressed against glass, then bushes, then trees. furniture sprang into the room from thin air. he made me cocktails that never ended. friends appeared as we continued to go further and further up. the apartment climbed a mountain. i was drunk. we reached the top floor, and the balcony doors slid open. mom was standing there with her apron on, cooking dinner.

///

"Daniel! Daniel, get the fuck out of bed!"

I groggily got up to the front door and let D in.

"You haven't been answering your calls, and it's five-thirty—what the fuck?"

"Sorry, we were having a really great date." I threw my phone to D. She flipped through the photos and finally stopped on one.

"Is this a photo of your mom?"

"Yeah, don't worry about it." I snatched the phone from her.

She started to clean my room and throw my clothes into the laundry basket. I jumped out of bed and made coffee. There was a big brown bag on the counter.

"I brought some dinner."

"I'm not hungry!" I yelled out.

"Are you making decaf?"

"No, it's regular," I lied.

///

we floated over mountains covered in wildflowers. you took my hand and showed me deep caves that we dived in, where gravity escaped so the dives never ended, stalactites turned into trees that flipped onto the other side of the earth. we landed on a beach where the water pooled in a circle. we jumped in a boat that spun in the centre, and we ate dinner at the bottom of the boat where there was a booth encased in glass. you said that we had a special date, and my mother walked in. i started to yell at you and asked why you brought her here—she wasn't supposed to be here. i yelled until you floated away, and i heard someone knock on the glass and scream my name

///

I felt hands shake me. It took a lot of energy to open my eyes.

"Oh, thank god. You've been asleep for two whole fucking days."

"That's impossible." I checked my phone; it was two days after I'd gone to sleep, and its memory storage was full. I scanned through the photos; they were countless—photos of us in deserts made of ice and rooms where the furniture was all over the walls and ceiling.

"Daniel, you have to stop this. People don't come back from this, and you haven't eaten in days."

I stared at the floor. I was so tired and just wanted to go back to sleep. "You gotta give this guy up. What do you even know about him?"

I flipped through the photos and couldn't respond.

"Does he even have a name?"

"He doesn't need a name—it's different. It's everything I've ever wanted."

"Great, then I can't wait to meet him and go on a double date with you two."

"You don't need to be a sarcastic bitch about it. It's just that my mom keeps showing up and ruining it for me."

"Daniel, I don't think that's the problem."

"No, it's definitely the problem. We're perfectly fine, and then my mom interrupts the dates."

"But isn't it nice to see your mom again?"

"It doesn't feel nice. It makes me feel fucking terrible. I need to figure out a way to get her to stop."

"Daniel."

"You don't get it."

She put some cookies on a plate next to my bed. "Just eat something. I have to head off, but I'll be back to check on you."

///

my childhood home expands to the size of the earth. we walk for days; we make flowers into dinner; we make candies out of the ocean; he proposes to me; he places the ring of saturn on my finger. we want to elope so we fly to vegas. we walk up the casino church aisles lined with slot machines, and my mother is at the end of the aisle waiting for me. i scream at her, "you don't belong here, you can't be here!" i cover her in fabric, and the fabric spins until it turns to ashes. the ashes float up, and they return with force at me until they spin and turn back into my mother. she is sad. she begs me to forgive her.

///

My face is stinging. I wake up to C standing over me in my bed, slapping me.

"What the fuck? Why did you wake me up?"

"Are you fucking insane? You're going to be hospitalized. You have to get up and eat something."

I got up. It felt as though I had only enough energy to sit up, and I fell to the floor next to the bed. C lifted me, carried me to the kitchen. My eyes were closing again. I could feel him shoving food in my mouth. I spat it out. His voice became faint, the dark circled me, and I let it.

///

the park outgrew its space there were sunflowers growing oversized into a forest he pulled me along a yellow brick path and we ran but our feet didn't move we ran and the earth moved beneath us until he pulled me up to a giant temple that reached up into the sky he said there and pointed to the top and i said yes and we walked to the entrance and it was an elevator up i felt a happiness i've never felt before my whole body was warm and then my mother grabbed his hand and i screamed at her i yelled that she can't be here and that this isn't about her and she just smiled and said she wasn't feeling good that she was sick then she said "i told you about handsome men" and he held her hand tightly and the doors to the elevator opened they walked in together and he smiled waving me in but i screamed that she couldn't come with us and he just continued to wave me in as the elevator doors closed and i watched as the elevator moved up and up until it was just a dot gliding into the sky

///

I could see a bright light. There was a familiar, sterile smell. My stomach painfully pressed against my ribs. I looked up, and D was sitting there with what was probably a cold coffee.

"My mom took him away."

"Of course she did."

"I'm really hungry."

D smiled. "I'm glad she took him away. He sounded like a real asshole."

DATE: LUVCUB

Hey

                                                                    Hi!

How goes it?

    ...

Hey?

Hi?

Cunt.

                                        Sorry, was just out for a bit.

Oh, lololol ☺ thot you were ignoring me

    ...

hey!

Hey?

Hi?

You know what, your loss! I am actually a really nice person, and you would
be lucky to have someone like me in your life.

I bet you just do this to everyone, playing your fucking gay games.

u r a fucking douche

fuck you

                        So sorry, I went to bed before responding!

Oh lololol

Hey, you wanna hang out later? ☺ ☺

                                        I don't think so.

Cunt.

                you have unread messages from a user who has blocked you

PHONE CALLS

It starts and ends with a phone call.

///

"She's gone."

I threw my phone against the window. I was speeding through traffic. It was pouring rain, and I couldn't see. Flying through red lights, I pulled over to catch my breath, but the words came again, "she's gone," and I sped through the suburbs until I made it to the house.

I burst through the doors and collapsed into my sister's arms. "She's gone." She assured me that we would be okay and kept repeating the words "We'll be okay" until the police needed more questions answered.

There were several people standing around. Someone ushered me into the living room, but I shrugged off their hands and ran into my mother's office and sat in her chair.

I could hear people talk. I pulled my hoodie over my head and pressed my hands against my ears so that all I could hear was the echo of my inner ears. I could feel people patting my head and rubbing my hoodie. It pulled on my hair.

The coroner walked in and asked me if I wanted to see her one last time. I looked up at her in confusion. I almost asked if they had the ability to bring them back to life once more before they take them to the morgue, but I kept quiet and shook my head. The coroner walked away, and I went back to closing my ears over my hoodie.

My oldest sister, Julia, came up behind me and whispered that I should come upstairs. I passed my mother's body, still lying in the middle of the living room. I averted my eyes, grabbed a liquor bottle from the cabinet, and ran up the stairs.

We sat around Julia's old room and shifted between looking at the floor and looking at each other, like each of us had a question no one could answer. My brother-in-law Kevin stole the liquor bottle from me and took a swig.

///

"Would you still love me if I was really fat?" He pulled his belly down to try and stretch away the few extra pounds gently covering his abs.

"Of course. I'd prefer if you were fat, then I wouldn't have to fight so much for your attention."

"Cute." He jumped over the couch and kissed my neck, flipped on the TV, and started to watch *Housewives*. One housewife was yelling at another housewife and each scene seemed to parallel the other.

L smiled and looked at me. I stared blankly.

"I know you hate these shows." He smiled apologetically like that would somehow change the channel. I began to clean the dishes, organize his apartment.

"Relax, come watch, it's terrible."

///

"I'm worried about your drinking."

"Frankly, I'm worried about your not drinking."

///

It was L's birthday. I asked him what he wanted, but he never responded with a real answer. I was broke, so I started to write him a fantasy novel in which we were all characters. In the story, I had gone missing, and his character was impervious to death.

After several hours of preparation, our friends arrived. K came from behind me and made a crack about my dating an older guy— "He's so old today."

"That's weird. I could have sworn he was eighteen at the most," I replied.

"Where is the fucker anyway?"

"In his room, changing. Trying to decide which white shirt with blue jeans he's going to wear today."

"He's so pretty." K sauntered off into the kitchen and began to pour drinks.

"To that old fag."

He walked in wearing a white shirt and blue jeans, his head held down, but his eyes looking up for approval.

"Yes, you're handsome, we get it," I mocked him. His sideways look turned into a smile.

///

The next morning, we didn't move the couch back. We left it an open space, where her body had lain. I was told that my father had pushed the couch back and moved her body to the floor to attempt CPR. She had taken a nap on the couch, and when the nap went on too long, my father called 9-1-1.

I went into her office and noticed the piles of paper she'd called "filing." There were harlequin novels stacked with year-end reports, invoices mixed with our old certificates from school. I started with the books, pulling them off the shelves and throwing them into a giant bag to be donated. I moved to the paper cabinet, organizing the paper according to size and colour, separating the bank statements from the craft paper, envelopes from the old photographs slipped in between. I organized her notes from most recent to oldest, most of which just had numbers or notes to herself—nothing I could decipher, but they still felt important. I opened three different bags filled to the brim with keys. There was no reason or rhyme to the keys, just piles of them—silver, gold, bronze, oval, square. I put them into one larger bag and set them aside.

My sister tried to pull me into the kitchen to have something to eat.

"Just coffee please."

///

We sat on the couch. He looked at me and began to cry. My body jumped toward him instinctively and I pulled his head into my lap. I stroked his hair and muffled my own tears to ask him what was wrong.

"I don't know. I just thought my family would be here," L said.

"But they said they couldn't make it, and you said that was fine."

"I thought it would be fine. I get weird around my birthday."

I didn't respond. I felt his head weigh heavily in my lap. I thought about Rogue from *X-Men*, the way she couldn't touch skin to skin without taking in all of the other person's energy.

We fell asleep with the rain hitting the window. When I woke up, he had moved to the bed. I switched over to the bed and we slept until the afternoon. When I woke up for the second time, he was making breakfast and singing and giggling to himself.

"How you feeling today, better than last night?"

"Yeah, why?"

"You were so upset last night."

He laughed, "No I wasn't."

///

I had a dream that went three levels deep: I dreamed that you got a second chance at life. So we flew off to the tropics, and you said it was your dying wish to go down a giant waterslide. So we climbed the stairs—you were tired but kept up—that led to more stairs, that led to stairs. Before we reached the top, we had to get into an elevator. You disappeared. I couldn't get into the elevator: it kept closing before I could enter. I woke up from that dream into the next and was paralyzed with grief, but remembered you were there. Then I woke up from that dream into the next and was paralyzed with grief, realizing it was a dream. Then I woke up and was paralyzed with grief.

///

"You never told your mom you're gay?"

"No."

"Why not?"

"She was so sick, and the doctors said she couldn't handle much shock. Her heart was so bad. I couldn't tell her. I was afraid that if I told her, it would break her heart, and I'd be the last person to break it."

"Oh, Daniel."

"It feels like all we ever do in this world is break each others' hearts."

///

It hit me while driving home. The sense that every breath was the last one. That while driving I would quickly fade out. That my breath was too short to sustain me. At any moment I would drop dead. I would lose control of the car. If I made it home, I would die on my bed, and no one would find me for days. My body would quickly turn to mush; my roommate would find me days later and be traumatized for life. There are only a few moments left. This is it. My last days, and the feeling of sorrow as the only memory before I go. What if I'm right, and there is nothing after death? What if I'm wrong, and the last moment you have is the memory that will be imprinted into you for eternity? What if I spend an eternity feeling like this?

I got home and pushed my face into the cold leather of the couch. I thought about how none of this was real, it was just a blip—this is what my dad called being "sick."

///

"It's like J not believing in dinosaurs," she said.

"You don't believe in dinosaurs?" I hollered.

"It just doesn't make any sense: who put them there?"

We looked over the different types of thank-you cards to choose from.

"How does an old man building a giant boat hoping to ship dinosaurs in them to escape a flood that lasted thirty days make sense then?"

"I don't know, it just does. Fuck off, Daniel."

We stared at the cards, each a nature scene, each a thank-you for lifting the body and helping to place her into the earth.

///

"People just die," my father said. "That's what they do."

///

The lights were blaring in my eyes. He was high on MDMA and trying to get me to drink more.

"C'mon, just have another drink."

I sat quietly, legs crossed. A young flighty kid walked up to him and started to flirt. I sat back and watched as he let the kid take his phone and add his number.

He asked me to go to the dance floor. Techno music began to quake inside my stomach. He ran off to dance when I declined. I stood there for half an hour until he returned. He mumbled something about hating this kind of music.

The flighty kid found us again and asked for his number, too drunk to remember he'd already had this exchange.

"Why didn't you say you had a boyfriend?"

"It just never came up," he shrugged.

///

"Sounds like your mother was always busy with work. So who mothered and fathered you?" Therapist was looking at her notebook.

"I don't know what you mean."

"Who were the parents, if your parents weren't around? What were you doing if they weren't home?"

"I dunno. I used to just play in our basement. It was a big, open cement space, unfinished with plywood and boards sticking out. I used to just stay down there and make up worlds." I stared at the floor. Something felt as if it was twisting me at both ends of my body and I couldn't move.

///

"Another round," he hollered at the server; he was five beers in. His eyes were glazed, his smile was moist from saliva. He looked at me. "Why aren't you drunk?"

"I'm just n—"

"M's here!" He waved him over.

M sat down and began to sarcastically chant, "Shots, shots, shots."

A round of shots arrived at the table, and we bit down limes to stifle the tequila. And shots arrived at the bar, and we bit down limes to stifle the tequila. And shots, shots, shots.

When the restaurant closed, we moved to the Cobalt—a former punk bar that had been renovated and taken over by a young gay scene—and shots were taken, and limes were bitten. He was too drunk and needed to go home. I was too drunk and needed to sleep. We walked home because we needed to sober up or the morning would be unbearable.

He mumbled something, and I couldn't understand him. He repeated, "You don't like me anymore."

"What?"

"You don't like me anymore."

The blood rushed to my head, and I became inexplicably angry. "The real problem is that I like you more than you will ever understand."

He stopped talking and walked ahead of me.

///

I dreamed that night that my mother was still alive. She was very sick, and I needed to take her up to her hospital room. I held her frail body, and she began to vomit on my jacket. She apologized. I told her it didn't matter. We kept going up and up and up. We couldn't get off the elevator. We knew the building was empty. She looked at me, confused. I told her that I was just dreaming. I told her that she wasn't sick anymore, but that she was already dead. She apologized.

///

I was in bed; I felt feverish. He jumped into the bed, threw his arm around me mechanically, as if his arm remembered how it would always fall around my chest. His breath shot a whiff of alcohol in my direction.

"What's wrong? You're mad. I can tell you're mad," he slurred.

"You don't like me anymore," I whispered.

His body shook. He went quiet. His arm slipped away from me. "I just can't do this anymore."

///

I slit another letter open and froze. My hand was stuck. My body couldn't move. I began to panic. S entered the office. I breathed deeply and closed my eyes until my arms could move again.

"You okay?"

"Fine," I lied, and ducked out toward the exit.

I pressed my forehead against the elevator as it slowly moved toward the ground floor. He was standing next to me, telling me I deserved this.

When the elevator doors opened, I ran to the bathroom, locked the door, and breathed into my palms until vomit took the place of air.

///

"I remember I used to sit under my mom's desk when she was working and would pull on the phone gently enough so it didn't fall from the receiver or her hands. I would wrap the curled cord around my finger then pull it tight like a finger trap ... I don't know, I can see it all, I can see all these things connecting. It's on a spectrum. These little moments—my mom, these memories—I can see them on a map in my brain. They connect, and it feels like too much for me."

///

When the files were all in order, I went to Staples and purchased file folders and as many sorting trays as I could find. I brought them back to the office and began to reorganize the shelves.

My sister brought in dinner, and I ate pizza while deleting old files in the computer and creating new folders for the old photos we'd uploaded to the computer. There weren't that many files, just some documents that she constantly reused. She seldom saved a file; every letter she typed on the computer was erased by the new one she wrote. There was a photo she had saved on her desktop: her with Julio Iglesias.

///

"I'm working on this story about after my mom died, and you're in it too, obviously. I just need to ask this because I don't even know if you remember it, but do you remember our first kiss?"

"Of course, we were at B's. I waited until the elevator doors closed and kissed you."

"We spent the entire day together, and you kept flirting with me. We had agreed we wouldn't date, that it was too soon for you. You spent the evening looking at me with a gleeful face, and your brother could see it too. We had Italian. My mother made us cannelloni, and I made us a cheese plate. Me and my mother made us a tiramisu: I wanted so badly to impress you. After dinner, we left. You, on the way to the elevator, pulled me in and kissed me. And we couldn't stop. We kissed all the way down the elevator. I didn't want to get out of the elevator. I didn't want to hit the bottom floor."

"How could you think I could ever forget that?" he asked.

"Because I needed you to be a monster."

"I thought you weren't supposed to write short stories about breakups?"

"I guess. My friend suggested that the only way a short story should end with a breakup is if the ex just flew away."

"You'd love that, wouldn't you?" he smirked. It turned into a frown.

I laughed.

///

I took the old family vacation photos that were in boxes and put them in binders according to date. We put duplicates into envelopes for family members whom I thought would enjoy them. My mother had even triplicated some photos. I sat at the desk and looked at the cheque statements, flipping through them in reverse so that her signature went from erratic to smooth.

When I finished organizing the last shelf in the office, I looked around for anything else that needed attending. I had gone through every cabinet, through the computer, and even through the attic. There were boxes of recyclables ready to go. There was nothing left to organize.

I collapsed on to the floor, unable to breathe. The words came again. "She's gone."

///

One day I went through her phone messages and emails. I was hoping to find anything I didn't know—a secret affair, someone I'd never met, anything—a narrative to keep her alive. There was nothing.

///

"I was reckless."

"I know. And I know you wanted to leave me, but there was no right time."

"You miss her?"

"When you left me, I would go and sit with her, and she couldn't really figure out why I was so sad all the time. She thought I was tired. And I was. I still hadn't told her about us, about you, about me." I began to inhale the dark. "Whenever I felt like the world was getting to me, I would go to her home and just lay on the couch. Now, when I feel like I'm falling apart, I'm afraid I will." I looked up to see him covered in tears. "Stop crying."

"I can't help it."

///

It was New Year's Day. I felt the pull from the night before, of MDMA taking me down. I spent the night at my ex-boyfriend's. You met him once—you liked him, not knowing he was more than just a friend. Not knowing that the bed we were moving out of your house would be shared by him in the future. When I woke up, he was showering and said he had to leave to be with another guy. I begged him to stay, taunted him for leaving me yet again, but he was always leaving, and I was always begging him to stay.

I felt the pull of MDMA again, the pull that is the opposite of the push into happiness that it can create, the one that creates love for everyone around you. This dark pull had you at the other end, had him leaving me once more.

I thought about how I couldn't remember the sound of your voice anymore. The oils of your skin no longer leave a scent in the air. That day

I brought your grandson into your room, he pulled at my beard, trying to understand why my face had hair at both ends and he began to giggle. I laid him on your bed and rested beside him. He grabbed at his feet and smiled; curling himself like a little crescent moon, he reached toward the bright lights, as babies do.

You'd never met him before. But I asked him to tell me a story. The way you used to. The way you asked me to tell you a story, before I learned the way narratives break.

///

"She's gone."

///

I was hanging my head over the bed. The phone was slick from the sweat of my hand. "I can't do this anymore," I said. I could hear L breathing deeply into the phone. "I love you," I added, knowing it was the only thing left to say.

"Okay." There was a long silence, and then a change in the silence, one that let me know he'd left.

I imagined the night he left, the night he admitted it was all over. I stared at his luggage. I held his hand as he cried himself to sleep. Then I imagined that he floated away. Not slowly, like a balloon in the sky, but all of a sudden, like gravity had reversed its pull on him and shot him straight into the sky. He never returned.

HAPPINESS IS HARD WORK

Me

My mom was showing me around. It was a party, but it wasn't a party that had to do with our family. Someone had purchased the house. My mom was just there as the current house owner to make sure everything went okay. I asked her why she'd sold the house, and she told me, "I figure it's too big for me and I should move closer to the hospital. That way I can be closer to you." I was happy with this decision. She asked if I wanted to meet the new owner and then introduced me to my ex and told me he'd bought the house. He and his new boyfriend would move in. They would take my old bedroom. My ex walked up to me and told me he was going to gut the house and completely remodel everything. Then I woke up.

Therapist

Do you believe that dreams mean anything?

Me

Yes and no. Just feels like it has to mean something if my ex is living in my dead mother's house.

Therapist

What do you want from these sessions? Why are you here?

Me

I remember when I used to like myself. Now, I don't know how that feeling works anymore. I remember when I felt awesome about myself. Now, it's like every thought I have about anything I do is so toxic. Yesterday at work, I thought about him and I went into paralysis: I literally couldn't move my body.

Therapist

I want you to write a letter to your ex and say whatever you need to say to him. That is your homework for this week.

***

Me

We were sitting around my childhood home, and my ex was sitting across from me with his sister. I asked if I could use the shower and they both claimed they'd need to use it soon. I began to feel furious that they had taken over my mother's home and screamed at the sister until I woke up in tears.

Therapist

You have to figure out how to remove him from the memory of your mother.

Me

I'm trying.

***

Me

There was this weird thing that happened last week. I was sitting there, and all of a sudden I had this feeling in my stomach. It was a deep gut feeling that I haven't felt before.

Therapist

And what was that?

Me

I could be happy, and everything was going to be okay.

Therapist

That's a good thing, no?

Me

It was right after that brief moment of happiness that I felt more dread than I have ever felt before in my life.

Therapist

Then that's it.

Me

What?

Therapist

I think this should be your last session. I don't think you need me anymore.

Me

But it was just a brief moment.

Therapist

Yup. That's kind of how it works. I'm here to get you to that point. The rest is up to you now. By the way, did you ever end up writing that letter to your ex?

Me

I did.

Therapist

And what did it say?

Me

I want you to move out of my mother's house. You don't belong there.

DATE: NOTALLICAN

Ryan walked right into the front entrance of the house, which was large, with pillars three storeys high. The front door was open and led into a cavernous entryway. A voice echoed from another room.

"I'm just in here."

Ryan went toward the voice. NotAllICan was preparing small canapés in the kitchen. Ryan stuck out his arm for a handshake. NotAllICan laughed and pulled him into a hug.

"You're much older than I thought." Ryan couldn't hold his irritation back.

NotAllICan laughed harder than before. "Well, if that's a problem, we can call it a night."

"No, no. It's fine. It's just, you look like your profile pictures, I just ..."

"I told you I was fifty-six."

"I know."

"Then why are you here?"

"I promised myself that I would say yes to anyone who asked me on a date."

"That's a bit of a Russian Roulette, no?"

"I guess."

"Has it been eventful?"

"Definitely eventful. I feel like I'm writing a memoir called *Bad Sex Date*."

He laughed. Ryan really liked his laugh.

"Let me pour you a nice drink, and let's move over to the couch. I hope you like these canapés I made."

"You like cooking?"

"Love it. Always thought I could be a chef if I wasn't so focused on my dancing career."

"You were a dancer!"

"Ballet dancer, to be specific."

"Well, you definitely have strong legs. Wait, you were able to afford all of this with ballet?"

"Oh, god no. I switched over to business. I got into developing businesses and then selling them off as soon as they became successful." NotAllICan rubbed Ryan's back. Ryan felt an immediate rush to kiss. NotAllICan lifted him onto his lap and felt Ryan's arms go up his shirt. Ryan felt like he wanted to bury himself in his body. NotAllICan picked him up and walked him over to the stairs.

"I'd carry you up my stairs, but I'm not that strong."

Ryan laughed.

NotAllICan was lying on his back, smiling up at Ryan who had just cum all over his stomach. NotAllICan laughed and Ryan started to laugh as well.

"Well, that was unexpected."

"Sorry, I don't know what happened there." Ryan rolled over and grabbed a nearby towel.

NotAllICan cleaned up and brought Ryan back downstairs. They finished up the leftover snacks and the wine.

"Would you be okay if I stayed the night?" Ryan asked.

"Well, that would break my rules. I don't let anyone stay overnight."

Ryan felt a chill roll over his body.

"No, no. It's not you. It's just a rule I have for myself. I really like being on my own. I spent a long time always trying to fit a relationship in my life and felt miserable, so to keep myself from dating, I just keep it simple."

"Doesn't that get lonely?"

"Sometimes. But I go on lots of trips, and I have a few best friends that I see often. They provide all the emotional support I need. And, well, men like you provide the other part. And I'm thankful for both."

"Oh, okay. Well, now I feel disposable."

"I don't think of it that way. I think of it like a way to fill my life full of love and lovely people. Some are just for a brief moment, some are for longer than that. I've been in relationships before and failed them very quickly on. Maybe you're more like me. What were you looking for?"

"Honestly?"

"Yes, honestly."

"I've never figured that out, and that's what scares me most."

LIKE BUFFY

"Remember that time we went around telling everyone we were brothers?"

A faint sound came from the phone.

"And then, finally, when everyone believed us, we kept making out near the pool? Strangely, some of them seemed cooler with the idea that we were incestuous brothers than gay men."

///

"Today I went shopping for the first time in two years. Remember how I used to wear out my clothes to nothing? Just strings and waistbands? I figured I would buy those nice jeans everyone is wearing, those really skinny ones. I found a good pair, bought them, and asked a friend if they thought they were too tight. They said no, so I went back to the store to return them and get a tighter pair. When I pulled them off there were all these wrinkles and marks on my skin from the pants digging in. I mean, I know I don't look like those guys with the nice bums, but I guess these help a bit. You never cared what jeans I wore."

There was a muffled sound in the receiver.

"You would like these jeans."

///

"I'm jealous of you. The way you fall in love so easily."

///

Rain rustles in the background.

"When you left, I didn't know what to do. I just drank every day until it was the next."

The phone is silent except for the faint sound of short breaths.

"I'm sorry either way. Anyway, we're all going to Lindsay's tomorrow. I hope to see you there."

///

"Stephen caught me masturbating last week. It was really embarrassing. The weirdest part was that he was mad because I left the dog in the room. I wasn't even thinking about it—his dog always sits in my room. What does a dog care if I masturbate anyway? He treats that dog like it's a human being that he'll have to take to school one day and then visit the counsellor when the dog is all, 'I have all these weird repressed sex problems because I used to watch my uncle masturbate.'"

He hears the phone being hung up.

"Oh, c'mon! I've told worse stories!" He throws the phone across the room.

///

"Caaaalling all my bad bitches," he slurs into the phone.

The phone is hung up.

"Whatever, asshole, you used to love that joke."

///

"You're always here, but I couldn't find you tonight. They kicked me out of the bar. I don't even get why. I didn't even have that much to drink. I'm fine. They don't even get it. You weren't here. I'm still outside. They kicked me out, I don't get it. Bunch of assholes. I'm here. Where are you?"

///

He attempts to hide the slurring in his voice. "You ever feel like sometimes you're just making it all up? Like, none of this is real, and we're all just inside our own heads? Like, all it will take is a single snapshot in time, and you'll realize that the entire existence you created is just a delusion? Like that *Buffy the Vampire Slayer* episode. Joss Whedon is like the Stephen Hawking of our time. No, wait, Stephen Hawking is the Stephen Hawking of our time."

///

"I'm starting to forget things about you, like the way you memorized lyrics so easily, or the way you flared your nostrils when you were happy. I forgot what your voice sounds like. Everyone says I should stop calling you, but I know you, the way you ignore linear timelines and narratives. At least, I think I remember that about you. Are you even there?"

///

"I'm not supposed to call you anymore."

///

"I thought of you today. I was leaving work, and I was crying, and this homeless guy asked me for money but I didn't have any. I was crying so hard, he gave me a hug."

///

"Sometimes I feel like maybe I'm Buffy the Vampire Slayer, and I'm like, walking around fighting demons in leather suits, and like, no one gets me."

There was a muffled sound in the receiver.

"You'd be Angel. Or Spike. Or that military guy nobody liked. Sometimes I feel like you're that military guy nobody liked."

///

"They say I shouldn't call you anymore."

///

The sounds in the phone were muffled; change clinked against the receiver and barely audible noises rose and lowered.

///

"I'm worried you aren't real."

///

"I thought about tongue-out smiley faces and thought of you. I ... I can't call you anymore. I'm going to try again, so I can't call you anymore."

///

There was static on the phone and music playing, but it was too faint to hear.

HIS BIRTHDAY IS NOT MARCH 7TH

1.

I'm going to die young, I tell Therapist. She gets mad at me when I say this, says that I can't predict that. I tell her that I am going to die young and that I will probably never fall in love, because statistically speaking, it's impossible—based on the fact that I will die young. Therapist says that anxiety is the reason I feel this way, and that it's not actually true.

She asks me if I've gone on any dates recently. I tell her about one guy. He's nice, and we've gone on several dates. I think they are dates, but we never call them that. If a date isn't called a "date," is it a date? She doesn't answer my question.

She asks how we met, and I tell her that I joined an online dating site as she'd suggested. I put in all of my preferences, completed several quizzes, took photos of myself, and posted them on my profile. It took me several weeks to finish the profile because I kept deleting it. She tells me that it sounds like I'm making progress.

Therapist asks why I haven't asked him out on a formal date. I explain to her that he appears to be happy, and I don't want to change that. She gets upset and asks if she can smoke in the room.

2.

He asks me if I want to stay at his place and watch movies. I ask him if this is a date. He doesn't hear me, so I just mumble something about liking movies.

3.

He has this thing about birthdays—he doesn't like to celebrate them. Therapist says that this could be from childhood trauma, but it's probably nothing and that a lot of people don't like birthdays. I ask him when his birthday is, but he won't tell me. I ask him if it's March 22nd, and he says no. I note in my phone memos that his birthday is not March 22nd. I thought it was March 22nd.

4.

I ask him if he is happy, and he says he's not sure. He asks me if I am happy, and I say I'm not sure—I don't really know if I've been the "happy" that everyone means when they say the word. I know I've felt joy, and I've felt many moments of joy chained together to form happiness.

His birthday is not March 3rd; I know this because his friend told me that wasn't the date.

He asks me why I fear being happy. I tell him that I will probably die young. He laughs hard and touches my hand. I ask him if this is a date. He says it is. I apologize to him for being weird. He laughs again.

I ask him if his birthday is the same as any celebrities', and he says yes, but doesn't tell me which.

5.

I go through my memos and put in all the dates his birthday is not. It's almost March, so I start to panic. What if I miss his birthday?

He makes me dinner. I ask if it's his birthday today; he laughs and says no. I ask him if, when he laughs, that feels like happiness. He frowns.

He tells me he doesn't feel happy the way other people seem to. He tells me that it's like there is a giant balloon of sad attached to him. Sometimes the balloon is very big, and it feels like it's lifting him away because he's too depressed—it seems as if the world is very far away and there's no way for his feet to reach the ground. He says sometimes the balloon is small and he drags it along; he feels good, but it's still there. The balloon is always there, he says, it just changes size and sometimes it's easy to go anywhere, but sometimes it's hard, and the balloon traps him in his room, too big to fit through a door. Or it's so large that it feels like he can't get back down to the · ground. He feels all alone, floating in the air.

6.

I stop answering his text messages and phone calls. Therapist asks why. I explain that I have a gut feeling about this. She says that my gut isn't always right. I tell her that something is wrong, and I think I should stop talking to him before things get worse—two sad people will probably make things worse for each other. She nods but she says she isn't sure she agrees. I cancel plans with my friend Ryan. He leaves me several texts asking if I'm okay. Ryan shows up at my apartment with candy and says I can't spend all week in my bed again, and he makes me take a shower. When I get out of the shower, Ryan tells me that I'm not going to die. I laugh. This is one of his tricks to get me to stop thinking about death. Ryan tells me I shouldn't give up on the guy just because of a "gut feeling."

7.

His birthday is not March 7th.

8.

He shows up at my house. I ask him to leave, but he asks why I haven't been returning his calls. It is now March 3rd. Today is not his birthday. He asks to come inside, and I make us tea. He's upset and explains to me why I should work with him on this. I get upset and ask him to leave. He doesn't.

He tells me that he hates his birthday because it always made him feel too visible; people would shine too much attention on him, and it made him feel small.

I touch his hand. I think about how big his hands are. I imagine myself as a three-inch person who could crawl into his hands and fall asleep. He would walk me around the world; I would see the mountains and the ocean from his hands. He would let me sleep on his neck at night. He would let me float away with him and his balloon.

He asks me why I stopped answering his calls. I tell him that I will die young and that I probably won't fall in love. That sad people shouldn't fall in love with sad people. That we will make each other sad and that we can't help each other.

I ask him if he thinks two sad people can be happy. He doesn't respond. I ask him if I made him happy, and he says that it's not that simple. I touch his face, and he pulls me into a hug, his soft belly pushing against mine. I tell him I like the way he feels in a hug. I tell him that I love the way depression has rounded his body, so perfect for a hug.

He kisses me for the first time, on a day that isn't his birthday.

I ask him how big the balloon is, and he says it's dragging behind him. I say that I will try my best to make the balloon small for as long as I possibly can, but that one day, he'll probably float away from me.

DATE: MONSTER

Monster knocked at the door. He was early. Ryan wasn't ready and snapped, "You're so fucking early!"

"Hello, it's me, from the dating phone application," Ryan could hear from outside the door.

"Okay, you're like early, girl scout, give me a fucking second," Ryan muttered.

"I'm sorry, what did you say?"

"I said I'm coming!" Ryan yelled not-so-politely. He rushed to the door, still in his towel and wet from the shower.

"Oh, wow. You're all wet."

"Yeah, sorry I was not expecting you to be so early."

"I'm sorry. I timed it so that I'd arrive just a few minutes after eight, but the buses were early and I waited several minutes down the street and eventually figured it might be better to come in early since it's raining again outside."

Ryan poured some wine for the two of them and quickly changed while Steve waited. When he returned, both glasses of wine were empty. Ryan refilled the glasses again. "You were thirsty?"

"Yes, very."

Ryan sat close to Steve and began playing with the hat on his head. "You know, you can take off your hat. It's not really needed inside."

"I'd prefer it on."

"You bald under there?"

"No! I mean, no. I have hair like you, but less greasy."

"Ouch." Ryan laughed.

"Sorry, I just meant in comparison."

"No, it's fine. I have thick skin. Dating has made me numb to things like that."

"I just get in a lot of trouble for the things I say, and I just—you're—uh, handsome."

"Thanks, you are too. There's something intense about you. Your eyes are stark black."

"Can I have more wine?"

Ryan poured more wine, and they finished those glasses quickly and poured out more wine until they were opening more than one bottle at a time. Ryan's head began to spin, and Steve was smiling with glazed eyes. Ryan flipped onto him and kissed him. Steve's eyes focused and pushed him off.

"What the fuck?"

"I just, I just want to take things slowly. Maybe we can just cuddle and watch *The Blue Planet*."

"What's *Blue Planet*?"

"It's great, it's a documentary on the different environments around the earth."

"Snooze. I'd rather just make out." Ryan jumped back onto him. "I can't stop staring at your eyes. They're so hot."

"Okay, but just kissing, please."

Steve felt Ryan open his shirt and push it past his chest. He could feel Ryan pulling at his skin, but the more Ryan kissed and moaned, the less he cared. He could feel his skin loosening. Ryan ripped his hat off and pulled his head toward him. His hands tore at the back of Steve's skin. It began to peel off. The fur under Steve's skin was cold to the touch. Ryan placed his cheek against Steve's, and instantly Ryan's skin stopped vibrating, it instantly cooled. Ryan continued to kiss him as the skin came off in long chunks. Unwrapping him from head to toe, Ryan pressed his naked body against the cold fur. Steve's wings unfurled and wrapped around Ryan's body. They slipped to the floor, the skin a mattress protecting them. Steve pulled off Ryan's clothes and felt his dick in his hands. Ryan instantly came onto Steve—it shot out all over Steve's furry body.

Ryan grinned from ear to ear and burst into a laugh. "I knew there was something intense about you."

Steve gasped for breath. "This isn't always who I am." He paused for a moment and looked at Ryan sitting on his belly. His wings were crushed under him. "I like being in my skin too sometimes."

Ryan threw a towel at him, and began picking up the large pieces of skin. "I'm pretty good at taking care of skin. I can help you. But don't put on your skin just yet."

"Why not?"

"We're gonna watch *The Blue Planet*."

Steve opened his wings, slid one under Ryan's body and curled the other around his chest, closing him in.

"Is this okay?

Ryan's heartbeat slowed down. He pressed play.

EVERYTHING IS AWFUL AND YOU'RE A TERRIBLE PERSON

HALIFAX

Hotels smell like old sweat or like ghosts who don't wear deodorant. Whenever I get into a hotel room I instantly think about all the times someone has had sex in that room; the place is basically a hotbed of forgotten orgasms.

"I have to hook up, at least once in my life," I said.

"Danny, you can do it." R lay on his belly, staring at the hotel drinks menu.

"You'll have to do it before the wedding. It's gonna be full of straight people. Well, straight-ish." C flopped onto the bed, almost rolling R off it.

I checked my phone for messages, still groggy after the long flight. I flicked on Grindr to see who was nearby. My phone beeped, and a message appeared.

You horny?

"Wait, I got a message. How do I respond? He's saying he's horny. I'm not really horny right now, but do I say I am? Is that stupid?"

I took the silence as a response that I was being stupid. Silence always equals stupid.

Yes, I am horny.

His response came in quickly. *Cool, bro, i'm close, wanna come over?*

I put my phone down as sweat covered my body. I picked it back up again a minute later. He'd sent me a series of nude photos.

"What did he say?"

"Um, he said maybe not tonight." I lied.

"You're lying."

"I'm lying."

The morning hit earlier than expected when construction work woke us up. Still jet-lagged, we tried to rest, but the pounding against cement created waves in our room. R got up quickly and started to yell at us to get up. He threatened to fart us out of the hotel room. We picked up our coffees, grabbed our bags, and jumped in the car.

"Should I have hooked up with that guy? He was actually really hot, and he's in this hotel."

"Danny, do whatever you want, but yes, you should have."

I flicked on Grindr and noticed his account was no longer there. "He deleted his account."

R grabbed my phone. "No, he blocked you."

DIGBY

The car rolled up to a large expanse of rock over the water. We walked around to see the ocean. C broke off branches and leaves for me to smell and occasionally handed me berries to taste.

"Is this poisonous?"

"Yes, Danny."

"Okay." I ate it. "It tastes like toothpaste."

"It's a wintergreen berry."

We spent the day in the car stopping at small towns along the way. Each town had cemeteries covered with small crosses blooming from the ground. Since we arrived too late in Digby to reach the ferry to St. John, we shacked up in a motel room. It was foggy, and the motel had a distinct murder vibe to it. Our room was at one end of the motel and smelled of a thousand visits. When we turned on the fan to circulate the air, it made a womping noise. We spent the evening getting drunk to the television series *Intervention* and invented a drinking game; whenever the addict on TV drank, we would drink.

ST. JOHN

The ferry to St. John squeezed us in. We spent the evening devouring food and beer. I didn't talk much and focused on my phone.

It was two in the morning and my vision was blurred from four pints of beer. I closed one eye to read the screen on my phone. He was a lawyer, good build, tall, looked nice. "Nice" is what I was looking for, but not too nice. There was a photo of him in a locker room, sweaty and hairy with a snarl on his face. This is also what I was looking for. I let my friends know exactly where I was heading, what he looked like, and that I would text as soon as I got there.

When I came down from the hotel room, there he was: locker-room sex guy. I adjusted the fantasy version of him slightly since he was wearing khaki pants. He was also holding two leashes that were attached to two very excited dogs.

"I figured we could walk my dogs, since they needed to get out today."

"I like dogs!" I yelled. Guys like guys who like dogs.

It was intensely foggy. I noted this: "It's intensely foggy." I said. "This is the stuff horror stories are made of."

He nodded as we walked up to our first destination. He pointed at the statue in the centre of the park and told me who he was and how he was important to the city. I stared at his mouth. Making the first move is important, but then I sat down because the beer was making my legs wobbly. The dogs took this as a sign that I wanted to be licked in the face.

"That's interesting," I said, focusing on the tongues of the dogs.

"C'mon, I want to show you more."

We walked for several minutes and stopped by the local market, closed because it was three in the morning, then went by three cemeteries, the fire station, and the law courts, which "had the largest spiral staircase in Canada."

We stopped at a church with bricks that looked blackened by scorching, like in an old fireplace, too thickly covered with ash to let the rain clean the stains.

"And this is where I got married," he said in a faltering voice.

"You have a husband?"

"Wife. And no, not any more."

I looked at the church, its one arena-style light blaring through the fog. I suddenly realized that I was cold, or, more realistically, I suddenly realized that I was sober. I started to think about beer. About the gentle dizzying effect of alcohol that made me feel warm in this cold.

"Can I ask what happened?"

"It was typical. We were high-school sweethearts. We had been dating so long that it felt like the right thing to do. Get married, that is. And me, being from a Catholic family, just went along for the ride. She quickly figured everything out before we could start having kids."

"Do you still love her?"

"I do."

We stood there quietly for several minutes. The church looked heavier now, more scorched than before. The fog was rolling over me, and I thought about beer again, then about the cold, then about the ocean.

"My mom died," I whispered.

"I'm sorry."

We walked back to the hotel as he pointed at more buildings and statues, explaining the importance behind them. When we arrived at the hotel, we could hear the drunken ramblings of local kids nearby. We stood outside, making small talk, and I waited for him to ask me back to his apartment.

"Scott!" the kids yelled. "Scott, you fucker!" They came closer until I realized that Scott was locker-room sex guy.

They asked him how he was doing. His face turned red. He quickly waved them off as their grunts and hollering fell back into the fog.

"Sorry, that was some friends."

He lifted his hand to shake mine. I jumped in for a hug and felt his hand squished against my belly.

"Your dogs are kind of annoying," I said.

"I know." He walked into the fog.

I walked back into the hotel, trying to be quiet.

"Did you get laid?" C asked, half asleep.

"No. Although I do know a lot of historical facts about St. John now."

"You're the worst at this."

We woke up early for the next stint of our road trip but decided to take a scenic walk around the city. I recalled as many facts as I could about the buildings. We passed by the church in which he'd gotten married. Our tour was the exact reverse of the previous night's, but the facts continued to come back to memory.

The fog slipped back into the ocean. I turned around to see a familiar building, the windows and doors towering above me, and I felt them pushing me back.

"This place has a large spiral staircase."

SALISBURY

Are you staying in town?

No, just passing by.

Oh, lol, it's so lonely here :(

P.E.I.

It was pouring rain, thick drops that clogged drains and disturbed the soil. There was about a bottle and a half of wine running through my blood, and in the corner of my eye, I could see the swings in the playground. Our small cabin was moist from the humidity.

"Fuck it!" I ran to the door, R following suit, and we rushed to the swings.

"What are you afraid of, Danny?!"

"Everything!"

///

We managed to drink enough to carry us into the evening. The wedding still trailed behind us as we rushed toward the beach. The light disappeared along with the road. We left our clothes on the grass and slipped into the ocean. It was too dark to see until the phosphorescence lit up our bodies. I could feel the gentle push and pull of the ocean. I went deeper.

"Don't go too far in, Danny."

"I'm not a baby, R."

"Yes, you are."

I imagined what it would be like to be pulled in. Would it be my lungs gulping up water, or would it be my arms, too tired, or would I want to be taken in? No one loves a dead body, just a memory that used to live in one. I felt my bladder reaching its maximum capacity.

"R, do fish bite your wiener if you pee?"

"No."

"Okay." As I peed into the ocean, the phosphorescence lit up, like I was a light magician throwing sparkles from my penis.

"My penis is shooting sparkles, you guys!"

R and C split off to the right. I walked further out into the ocean, scooped up water, and poured it out. I walked further out and thought about the way the ocean could consume me. I could keep walking out into the ocean and it would scoop me up. I felt joy.

///

"What are you afraid of Danny?!"

"Everything!"

R stopped swinging and looked at me as I kept attempting to swing higher and higher.

"You know you're okay, right?"

"I don't feel okay."

"You're doing great."

"When will I stop saying to myself, 'Everything is awful'?"

"You know a thing or two about beginnings and endings. Just enjoy what you had and not what you're missing."

"That's the 'shrooms you took talking."

"No—well, some of it, sure."

We kept swinging until the neighbours came out. We were making more noise than I thought.

HALIFAX

I lifted up a package of coffee. "Hey, they have Titanic-themed coffee!" R grabbed the bag of beans. "Weird."

"Titanic coffee: literally drown in flavour."

"Danny!"

"Sorry. Titanic coffee: for that deep, sinking roast."

"You're a terrible person, Danny."

"Just one more. Titanic coffee: for when you hit that iceberg in your day."

R shook his head and walked away. I thought of several more and rolled the words "terrible person" back and forth in my head. I thought about how valid it felt. I was a terrible person. I'd be better as a ghost, or a monster, or a memory.

"Titanic coffee: try it *ice cold*!"

///

We were three pitchers of beer in. We'd met a stranger we referred to as Porn Beard. He was going through his tattoos, half of which he'd done himself. His knee tattoo was geometric but awkwardly handled. He had a Courtney Love tattoo. He talked about how much he hated Halifax and wanted to get out of there. He recounted his boyfriends, showing us each of them on his Grindr account. One guy was a part of a three-man relationship, which he had been kicked out of. Another was a guy who tried to kill him using a glass bottle. His stories became less and less reliable. I stopped paying attention when the lies became too obvious and turned to my phone.

"Okay, this guy looks pretty good. Or this guy!" I flipped through my phone, showing them picture-by-picture.

"Danny, at some point you just have to pick a dude." C punched me in the leg.

"What if one of them is a serial killer? What if I'm the first in a series of murders, and they call him the Grindr killer? I'd be so embarrassed."

"But you would be dead."

"Yes, but no one would feel bad for me—they'd just think, *Well, he's an idiot who went to some stranger's house, so he deserves it*."

"Sometimes you're really dumb for a smart person."

R stole my phone from my hand. C looked over his shoulder and giggled.

"There." R handed me my phone.

I went into the last conversations, and to each person he had texted the words, "This place is a dick desert. How does anyone get laid here?" A cold sweat covered my face.

He took my phone again, typed a few words, handed it back.

"There! This guy, thirty minutes."

I turned to Porn Beard and showed him my phone. "Have you ever seen this guy?"

He shook his head.

"Perfect!" said the seven beers I'd had. I walked out of the bar, and a cab arrived in front just in time. It felt as if everything was sliding in place. This was a perfectly choreographed musical, and I was swinging my way up to someone's apartment.

I opened the door; I didn't let him talk for more than a few seconds before I dived into him. In moments we were in his bed. I thought about wishing that I was still back at the bar drinking beer. *I left a whole beer at the bar. It was pretty good. I think it was an IPA. It was so frosty and delicious. I wonder if R or C drank it. Or if that weird guy did. What was his name? Porn Beard. No, that was his Grindr name. Either way, I hope he didn't drink my beer. I still can't believe he tattooed his own leg, or that he had a Courtney*

Love tattoo. I really like "Celebrity Skin," that was a great song.

"Are you okay?"

"Sorry, I was ... yeah, all good."

I closed my eyes and reached for his body, but he slapped my hand away forcing me to lay back. I focused on finishing as quickly as possible. He kissed me and said, "You can't stay over, I have an early day tomorrow." I nodded and rushed out.

"You're back soon." C looked disappointed.

"Yup. Unrelated question: What size penis would you consider to be a micro penis?"

"Danny, you're an asshole." C got out of bed to put me in a headlock. "How did you even have time for sex that fast? You didn't even go, did you?"

"I'm not judging or anything, I just want to know what you would consider small for penis size?"

"You're a monster."

"Not a monster, but definitely a terrible person."

The next day I expected a message, but nothing. I wasn't sure if you thanked someone for a hookup or at least acknowledged it happened.

We were in the Halifax Citadel museum, and R and C were trying on colonial costumes and taking photos when I stopped and looked at my feet with intense concentration.

"Come on, Danny. Put on a maid's outfit."

"No, those things are gross."

We moved toward the open square of the Citadel. Several people playing historic characters were leading tours. A man kept asking one of the tour leaders what their life was like, and he attempted to answer, but his cell phone went off and he answered it.

I turned to C. "Would it be rude to ask the guy I hooked up with last night what his name is?"

***

I scooped up the ocean water and poured it out. I walked further out into the ocean. Bioluminescence lit each step. I looked over to see R and C's bodies outlined by the night's sky. I moved in deep enough that my head was being enveloped in the water. I couldn't feel the ground, and the taste of salt dribbled into my mouth. I thought about how easy it would be to let me body drift off. How simple an action death could be. Darkness pooled around my eyes.

"Come back, Danny, you're too far out."

I dropped down into the water, let my feet hit the ground to kick back up and broke through the water to inhale. I swam back toward the beach, the awful ocean sliding off my back.

everything was okay. you were here

ACKNOWLEDGMENTS

Thank you to those who read earlier versions of this book, including Zoe Whittall—thanks for your notes. And thank you to the shame club—Clayton Dach, Katharine Guerin, and Jonathan Turner—for reading drafts of many of these stories.

To my writing soul-mate, Dina Del Bucchia, thank you for taking this book to places I couldn't imagine, for your suggestions, your book recommendations, and your solidarity in rage.

Thank you to Jen Sookfong Lee, Vivek Shraya, and John Early for writing kind things about the book. Thank you to Arsenal Pulp Press for taking this book on—Brian, Robert, Susan, Oliver, and Cynara (for both her friendship and support). Truly a dream team.

Thank you to my family and friends for your support. Thank you to new additions to the family, the Liedmans and Julie, for your help and for endless Prosecco.

To my future husband Gabe; thank you for walking out of my dreams and into my life.

This book was written for Tina, my late sister who passed when I was very young and for my mother Simira, whom we lost recently. I'm sorry if I wake you in your sleep.

And, as always, thank *you*, for reading this book.

Daniel Zomparelli is the Editor-in-Chief of *Poetry Is Dead* magazine and co-podcaster at *Can't Lit*. He also co-edits *After You*, a collaborative poetry project. He is the author of the poetry collections *Davie Street Translations* and (with Dina Del Bucchia) *Rom Com*, both published by Talonbooks.